"You want me. You can't hide it," Troy said smoothly

"Your lips are pursed, as if you're thinking of being kissed. Of kissing back," he continued. "Of using your mouth for something other than talking...."

"Pursed lips can also be a sign of attitude," Venus countered weakly.

He nodded. "Oh, honey, there's no question you've got miles of attitude. But it's not your attitude at work when your lips are full and ripe and parted like that. It's another part of Venus altogether."

Yeah. The empty, aching part that needed to be filled by him. She closed her eyes, desperately trying to relax.

"Even your legs are shaky," he teased, running his fingers along her thigh.

Her eyes flew open. "I didn't think touching was part of this demonstration," Venus said between ragged breaths.

"It's not. I don't have to touch you to know how badly you want me." He moved his hand again, the tips of his fingers scraping ever so delicately across the curls concealing her womanhood. "Though if I did, I think we'd find out quickly just how much you do...."

Dear Reader,

Welcome to THE BAD GIRLS CLUB! I think every romance reader has come across a book that has a great "bad girl" secondary character—a woman whose story they'd like to read. But it sometimes seems difficult to envision that slightly outrageous, possibly shady best-friend type as a heroine. Thankfully, in Temptation, anything's possible!

I loved writing about Venus Messina in my March 2002 book, *Into the Fire*, and many readers apparently loved the plucky redhead, too. The problem was finding just the right hero to be her match. When I finished writing my June book, *Two To Tangle*, I realized I'd found that hero—Troy Langtree. Because who better to bring down a very wicked woman than an even more wicked man?

This book was such fun to write. Venus is my kind of woman—gutsy, strong, funny, sexy and yet, believe it or not, I think she's the most vulnerable heroine I've ever written. And what can I say about Troy? I *adore* him, wicked rogue that he is. The icing on the cake was working with two of my other favorite Temptation authors—Julie Elizabeth Leto and Tori Carrington. The "bar scene" in *Wicked & Willing* should give you a little taste of what's to come.

Hope you enjoy hanging with the bad girls....

Leslie Kelly

Books by Leslie Kelly

Leslie Kelly
WICKED & WILLING

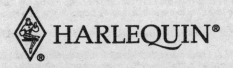

HARLEQUIN®

TORONTO • NEW YORK • LONDON
AMSTERDAM • PARIS • SYDNEY • HAMBURG
STOCKHOLM • ATHENS • TOKYO • MILAN • MADRID
PRAGUE • WARSAW • BUDAPEST • AUCKLAND

To Julie, Lori and Tony...
terrific writers, even more terrific friends!
Thanks for making this project
such a wonderful experience.
And to my readers. Thanks for hanging in there
with me for another wild ride.

ISBN 0-373-69116-5

WICKED & WILLING

This edition published by arrangement with Harlequin Books S.A.

® and TM are trademarks of the publisher. Trademarks indicated with
® are registered in the United States Patent and Trademark Office, the
Canadian Trade Marks Office and in other countries.

Visit us at www.eHarlequin.com

Printed in U.S.A.

1

"WHAT WOULD YOU SAY if I told you it's possible you're the long-lost granddaughter of a millionaire?"

Venus Messina snorted as she twisted the cap off a bottle of Bud, then flipped it into the trash with her thumb. She didn't even look over her shoulder at the uptight old windbag whom she'd dubbed Mr. Collins—Tom Collins—since that was his drink of choice. He sat at the end of the bar and had been trying to engage her in conversation since the moment he arrived.

Granddaughter of a millionaire. Right.

Lemme guess...my Granny is Miss Manners. Cause everyone can see I'm just like her. She chuckled under her breath.

The man persisted. "...and his direct heir?"

Though his voice grated shrilly over the noisy chatter in the crowded room, nobody even glanced over in curiosity. It was late into Happy Hour on a hot Friday night in June, and everyone knew Friday nights in an Irish pub were as good a place for outrageous stories and high drama as any movie theater.

Tonight was the third time this week the man had parked himself here at Flanagan's, her foster uncle's bar, where she'd been working until she could find a full-time job. The first night, the man had been so quiet she almost hadn't heard his drink order. He'd looked as out of his element as a nun in a strip club. Not so much in the way he dressed, though. After all, Flanagan's catered to a lot of ambitious, wealthy businesspeople who spent their days bowing down to the almighty dollar in one of the many huge office buildings in downtown Baltimore.

No, he didn't look out of place because of his pricey dark suit, which even Venus could tell probably cost more than she made in a month—or more than she *had* made in a month when she'd actually been employed full-time. Instead, it was his stiffness, the upturned tilt of his pointy chin, the way his nose flared in that irritating way when somebody stepped too close. The way he combed one long strand of graying hair over the top of his head to hide a bald spot, because, after all, rich people were much too refined to ever wear something as gaudy as a toupee.

Nope, she couldn't say she liked Mr. Collins, even if he was a damn good tipper.

"Are you even going to answer me, young lady?"

The imperious tone said he'd given up on easy friendliness, something he'd tried last night and failed at miserably. Mr. Collins's face looked like it was going to crack from his smile—obviously he didn't use it very often.

Tonight he'd skipped friendly and gone for nosy. He'd been trying to engage her in conversation and had been asking way too many personal questions—none of which she'd answered, of course. After she'd spent the past hour ignoring everything he said that wasn't prefaced by the standard, "Bartender, get me a...," he'd finally blurted out his ridiculous millionaire comment.

"Well?" he prompted, impatiently tapping his perfectly manicured fingers on the top of the pitted, sticky bar.

Sliding the bottle of Bud and a Fuzzy Navel—a disaster of a drink if ever there was one—to the yuppie couple seated at the bar, she muttered, "I'd say somewhere a village is seriously missing its idiot."

Yuppie man grinned. His date, with the pisspoor taste in drinks, gave Venus a quick frown, warning her away from spoken-for territory. *As if, lady.* Guys in ties were definitely not Venus's bag these days. As a matter of fact, she'd lately sworn off all men in general. Her last relationship had burned her—*badly*—leaving her not only brokenhearted, but jobless to boot.

Besides which, Venus had decided thirty was too old to keep playing the field. She looked forward to her thirtieth birthday the way a condemned prisoner looked forward to the executioner.

Thirty. Less than a year away. *Now, doesn't that suck?*

Venus didn't so much mind the number. She *did* mind not being where she'd thought she'd be by age thirty—in a great job, a stable relationship, a house, maybe even with a couple of rugrats running around. Her upbringing had made her desire *The Brady Bunch* life as an adult.

At the rate she was going, she'd be lucky with *The Osbournes.*

"It would behoove you to take a brief break and speak with me," Mr. Tom Collins said, still red in the face from her previous comment.

"Behoove?" She paused to finish pulling a draught of Guinness, complete with the requisite "G" swirl of foam on top. She pushed it toward the waitress, and grinned as Janie rolled her eyes behind the annoying man's back. "It would also behoove me to earn my paycheck, don'tcha think, Janie?"

The woman snorted. "You call what that cheapskate Joe pays us a paycheck?" Venus took no offense. Janie was Joe's on-again, off-again girlfriend. This week they were off-again.

Besides, Janie was right. The pay was pretty abysmal. It was the tips that had kept her clothed and fed for several months. For some reason, the regulars at Flanagan's seemed to like Venus's caustic wit and in-your-face attitude. Plus, she made a damn fine Bloody Mary, if she did say so herself.

But bartending wasn't exactly her dream job. Up until eight months ago, Venus had had the job she'd always hoped for, complete with the kind of salary that had enabled her to actually open a savings account. Starting out in the typing pool of a financial company right out of high school, she'd worked her way up for ten years. She'd scraped and studied, taken college night courses when she could. She'd put in long hours and kept the right attitude, including keeping her mouth shut when the occasion warranted it. Eventually she'd ended up in management in the HR department.

Then she'd been stupid enough to let down her guard, to get involved with Dale, one of the executives in the company. She'd fallen in…well, not love, but at least infatuation. He'd fallen in lust. Unfortunately, she'd gotten over the infatuation a little sooner than he'd gotten over the lust. When she'd broken it off, he hadn't been pleased.

In fact, he'd been so displeased, Dale had made sure Venus ended up on the unemployment line three months later.

Hence, her dislike for guys in ties.

Without a college degree to go with her experience, Venus had simply been unable to find a new job—unless she wanted to start all over again at the bottom of the ladder.

She might reach that point. If she hadn't had this job at Joe's place to fall back on, plus the remainder of that nearly empty savings account, she probably already would have. But holding out for a better-paying job wasn't just about taking care of herself. She needed to make enough to get back to helping Ma. Her foster mother had insisted she was doing fine, but Venus knew more than most the way Maureen struggled. Until her layoff, Venus had managed to send enough back to Trenton to make a real difference for the four kids currently living in her old home.

She wanted to be able to do so again. Soon.

"Imagine not having to worry about a paycheck," the man said, sounding almost desperate. "Please, Ms. Messina, give me a few minutes of your time." The word "please," and the urgency in his voice, made her pause and really look at the man.

"Go ahead, V," she heard from behind her. Glancing over her shoulder, she saw the sardonic look on her uncle Joe's craggy red face. "And if you're a millionaire heiress, don't forget who taught you to ride a bike."

"That woulda been Tony Cabrini, the boy in 6A," she replied with a saucy grin.

Joe wagged his index finger at her. "And who taught you how to deal with Tony Cabrini and boys like him when he got fresh on your fourteenth birthday?"

Venus fisted a hand and put it on her hip. "Ma did."

"Well, who do ya think taught *her* that knee trick, hmm?"

Laughing helplessly, she said, "Okay, okay. Thanks for teaching her the knee trick, Uncle Joe."

Not that she'd ever used it on Tony Cabrini. The last time she'd seen him, her knee definitely was *not* the body part she'd reacted with when he "got fresh." She'd lost her virginity to Tony in the laundry room of their building when she was sixteen.

Venus still had a real fondness for the spin cycle.

"Now, take a break," Joe said. "You can use my office." He turned toward the stranger. "Don't try nothing funny. You try to run a con on her and I'll make sure you have to drink your vodka through a straw for the rest of your life."

Venus gave Joe a quick hug, noting his start of surprise. Though not a real blood relation, he was as close as any uncle one could want. His sister, Maureen, had been Venus's foster mother since age eight. She remembered looking forward to Joe's visits to Jersey the way she'd look forward to Santa in December—even if Santa had usually brought only sensible clothes and donated secondhand toys, rather than the Barbie stuff and play makeup Venus had asked for.

Heck, when she thought about it, Joe's visits were probably more entertaining than Santa's anyway. Joe had taught her to play poker when she was ten. He'd taught her to spit like a boy when she was twelve. He'd taught her how to fake a fever to avoid a big exam when she was fourteen.

He'd also taught her that being poor was nothing to be ashamed of, and used himself as an example of how you could get what you want if you were willing to work for it.

She'd never forgotten the lesson.

Joe had also been the one who helped Venus when she'd come to Baltimore looking for a job right out of high school. And he'd been her closest family member ever since.

"Okay," she said over her shoulder to her impatient customer. "You've got five minutes."

Leading him through a swinging door, Venus walked into the cement-floored storage room, piled high with boxes and crates, broken bar stools and lined with shelves full of premium liquor. At the back of the room was the desk Joe referred to as his office. Sitting in Joe's well-worn chair, Venus leaned back, crossed her arms over her chest, and watched as the stranger sat in the metal folding chair opposite her. "Now why don't you tell me who you are and what the hell it is you want?"

Though he stiffened, she didn't apologize. He was on her dime. And if he didn't like her attitude, that was too damn bad. To Venus, attitude was everything.

"My name is Leo Gallagher," he finally said. "And, to confirm, you are Venus Messina, born in Trenton, and your parents are Trina O'Reilly and Matt Messina?"

"So they tell me, not that I know for sure since I never laid eyes on my father," she said. Then she narrowed her eyes. "Any particular reason you've been checking up on me?"

He ignored her question and mumbled, "The hair is a surprise. But the eyes, that deep green..."

Venus watched as he looked her over again, knowing what he saw—a tall redhead with a big mouth and the kind of figure that could turn horny men into drooling idiots and jealous women into shrews. Venus had long since stopped feeling self-conscious about her height or her very curvy figure. But she began to fidget as the man continued to study her.

"Your parents weren't married."

It wasn't a question, but she answered anyway. "Nope. Shocking, huh? My mother used to joke about how awful her name would have been, Trina Messina."

He ignored her sarcasm. "You never knew your father, and lost your mother to cancer when you were eight."

Venus clenched her back teeth, fighting the impulse to

stand up and walk out of here. "What do you want?" she bit out.

He seemed to sense her patience was nearing its end. "Ms. Messina, I believe your father, who called himself Matt Messina, may actually have been my cousin, Maxwell Longotti, Jr."

Her heart beat a little faster, but Venus took a deep breath, ignoring it. "Why?"

"My cousin left my uncle's estate in Atlanta thirty years ago, determined to make it as a stand-up comedian. He stayed in New York for a while, using a stage name—Matt Messina."

Her heart quickened even more. "My mother met my father in New York, but she never mentioned a stage name." *However, she did say he'd made her laugh like no one else she ever knew.*

"She might not have even been aware of it. I don't believe they could have known each other very long. He was in New York City for only a few weeks, and then he went out to California."

Unable to help it, she asked, "Where is he now?"

"He was killed in a car accident less than a year later."

Venus closed her eyes, angry with herself for allowing a tiny spark of hope to burn for the briefest moment. "Oh."

"He planned to return to New York, but was going to stop in Atlanta first to try to make amends with Uncle Max. They'd parted rather bitterly, you see. He phoned, said he wanted to mend fences. Something amazing had happened, he said. Something that made him reevaluate the importance of family."

Like finding out he had a baby with a woman he'd had a fling with back in New York? She thrust the thought away.

"The next day we heard Max had been killed. When

his father went out west to settle things, he found a card in Max's apartment. It simply said, 'Congratulations, Daddy.' Inside was a photo of a baby with the name Violet written on the back."

"My name's Venus," she immediately countered.

The man shrugged, as if unconcerned. "Possibly a nickname? Perhaps your mother changed her mind?"

"No *way* would my mother name me Violet. Besides, I think I would know my own name."

Leo glanced away, not meeting her eye. "Are you certain of the name on your birth certificate?"

"I've never seen it. There was a robbery at my foster mother's place back when I was in high school and a bunch of papers got stolen."

He raised a brow.

"But," she insisted, "my driver's license, social security card and school records all say Venus. I think by now somebody woulda figured it out if I'd been using an illegal name."

"Perhaps. But no matter." The man—who thought he could be her what...uncle? Second cousin?—smiled thinly. "The point is, there is enough circumstantial evidence to think it is *possible* you are my cousin's illegitimate daughter."

She remained silent, absorbing his claim. Her heart no longer raced, and she didn't tremble with excitement. If she hadn't just been told Max Longotti Jr. had died nearly thirty years ago, perhaps she could have allowed herself a moment of hope...a moment of that familiar longing to find out who her people were. Now, she felt only anguish. Whether the man spoke the truth or not, she was no closer to having a real father now than she'd ever been.

Deep down, she prayed he was wrong, this so-called

relative. She'd long imagined her real father living a great life, being the great guy she liked to think he was. She'd pictured his happiness when he'd learned about the existence of his daughter, who he must never have known about since he hadn't come for her when her mother died. Her mother told her she'd tried to contact him about Venus's birth, and she'd never stopped believing he'd return to them.

But what if he hadn't gotten the news? Messages got lost. Phone numbers changed. Postmen went postal and didn't deliver the mail. Her father could very well be out there somewhere, living his life, as wonderful as her mother had said he was.

No. Venus didn't want to imagine him dead. Not now. Not ever.

"Okay, Mr. Gallagher," she said as she stood and squared her shoulders. "You've said what you wanted to say. It's a nice fairy tale, but I don't believe it. My name is not Violet. Matt Messina is not exactly an unusual name. New York's a big city. And I think it's time for you to leave."

His jaw dropped and his eyes widened. Obviously he'd expected her to fall at his feet in gratitude. Right now she wished she'd never laid eyes on him.

"B-but, you have to admit it's possible," he sputtered.

"Why? What difference does it make if the man is dead?"

"Well," he said, "because I want you to come to Atlanta to meet your grandfather."

She began to shake her head. Accepting this Longotti character as her grandfather would mean accepting that her real father had died decades ago. It would mean accepting she really had no parents and the father she'd fantasized about all her life had been in his grave before she took her first steps.

No thank you.

"And I will pay you a great deal of money to do so."

Venus paused. Then she slowly lowered herself to her chair.

TROY LANGTREE sat in his new office at Longotti Lines, nodding with satisfaction at the tasteful decor and the magnificent view of downtown Atlanta off the balcony. His office at his family-owned department store in south Florida had been just as nicely appointed, but its view had been of swaying palm trees and bikini-clad beach goers.

"Well, that had its benefits, too," he murmured with a wry smile. Still, he found himself appreciating the look of Atlanta. The skyline spoke of big-city energy and excitement. In the week he'd lived here, he'd found himself growing energetic and excited, too.

He still couldn't quite believe he was here. His move to Atlanta had been rather a shock, even to him. If someone had asked Troy a year ago where he saw himself on the day of his retirement, he would have firmly replied that he'd still be heading up the Langtree store chain in Florida. He'd never pictured himself doing anything else.

After his father had retired six years ago, he'd worked with his twin brother, Trent, until they both realized Troy liked the store and Trent hated it. When Trent struck out on his own to start a landscaping business, Troy had moved into the executive position with ease. He'd enjoyed his job, and if he sometimes felt bored, closed-in, well, he'd had other outlets to pursue in his off-hours. Mainly outlets of the female variety. As a wealthy, and, to be honest, attractive bachelor, he had never lacked for female company.

But about a year ago, his well-laid plans began to wrinkle. His brother's marriage had been a surprise, though a pleasant one. Watching Trent go crazy over his wife, Chloe, Troy had wondered, for the first time in his life, if he might ever meet a woman who could turn him into a complete idiot, like his brother had become.

"Doubtful."

His sister-in-law's subsequent pregnancy had thrilled the entire family, Troy included. It was, probably, why he'd been foolish enough to get briefly involved with someone not at all his usual type. By dating a friendly, personable young woman who reminded him a little of his brother's wife, had he been subconsciously trying to follow Trent's lead?

Maybe.

Whatever the reason, it had ended in disaster. Because, for once, Troy had gone out with a woman who hadn't played the dating game. She'd fallen and fallen hard. Troy hadn't.

Oh, sure, he'd liked her. She'd been nice and attractive. And she'd bored him beyond belief.

Their breakup had devastated her, and she'd definitely let him know about it. Troy had never meant to hurt her. He'd certainly never made any promises and they'd only gone out a few times. Hell, they'd never even *slept* together—which should have been his first indication something was wrong.

Looking back, he couldn't even fathom why he'd thought he could be interested in someone who didn't make him crazy with lust from the first time they met. Love might be the greatest thing since the invention of the wheel, but if it wasn't accompanied by a serious case of the hots, Troy didn't think it would ever be for him. Any woman with whom he fell in love would have to inspire some immediate thoughts of hot, sweaty bodies and long, erotic nights before she could ever inspire images of diamond rings or whispered promises.

"It will never happen," he'd often told himself, especially after that last dating disaster.

In any case, the damage had been done. For the first time in his life, he'd hurt someone who hadn't deserved it.

Lots of women had called him a heel over the years, but this was the first time he'd ever actually felt like one.

Worst of all, the situation had made him cautious about his relationships with women. He hadn't so much as wanted to kiss one in a good three months! That was pretty long for a man who hadn't gone without *sex* for three months since losing his virginity at fourteen to his grandmother's housemaid.

His twin said occasional breaks from sex could be good for a man. Frankly, Troy thought he'd rather lose an arm than his sex drive. "You can teach yourself to write with your other hand," he mused. But you couldn't teach other body parts to have orgasms.

Still, even his suddenly barren love life couldn't compare with the upheaval in his career. The job in which he'd felt so secure had suddenly disappeared.

I think you're crazy, Dad.

After six years of retirement, his father had decided he wanted his job back. He had to hand it to his old man. Most fifty-eight-year-olds who'd had a minor heart "episode" would take it as a sign to slow down. His father had decided his early retirement was going to kill him, and that he'd been much healthier when working. So back to Florida he and Troy's mother had come. Back to the store. Right into Troy's job.

His father certainly hadn't pushed him out. They'd be partners, he'd insisted. But when Troy had thought it over, he'd realized he was being given a chance to do something he never thought he would—go outside the store, maybe move somewhere else altogether, try another line of work.

Freedom from Langtree's had been shocking—but also intoxicating. He'd finally understood some of the choices his twin had made. Though, God knew, he'd never fathom Trent's delight in planting bushes or mucking around in fertilizer.

Fate had stepped in to make his decision a simple one. Max Longotti, an old friend of his late grandfather, had told Troy's grandmother he was thinking of selling his nationally known catalog company. He wanted the Langtrees to consider buying it. To that end, he asked Troy to come work with him at his Atlanta headquarters for a few months, so the board could get to know him before Max asked them to vote on the sale.

Troy had leapt at the chance. He'd closed up his beach-front condo and driven to Georgia. Max Longotti, a crotchety old soul who reminded Troy of his grandfather, had welcomed Troy into his own home until he could find another place. He'd be moving into a furnished apartment in a few days. Until then, the Longotti estate was quite comfortable—if large and rather deserted.

One thing Troy had learned so far during his brief stay in Atlanta...Max Longotti was a lonely man. A rich, lonely man who seemed surrounded by scavengers just waiting for him to kick the bucket so they could sink their claws into his money. Troy shook his head in disgust.

Remembering Max had mentioned he'd be in late in the afternoon due to a doctor's appointment, Troy glanced at his watch, noting it was nearly four. He should have just enough time to read over the marketing projections for the latest sales circular before meeting with Max at the end of the day.

He reached for it, but froze when something else—a bright flash of red outside—caught his eye.

A woman. "Who the devil..." He stood, walking toward the sliding glass door which lead out to the small balcony. A nice touch, the balcony. Troy had become accustomed to sitting outdoors when he had reading to do or reports to peruse.

Obviously no one had come through his office, so the intruder had to have come out the other door, which exited off Max's. Knowing Max hadn't yet arrived, he wondered why the older man's efficient secretary had left the woman alone. And, more importantly, why was she here to begin with? Watching her out the glass, he doubted she was here on business.

The woman had to be tall. She sat in one of the two tasteful, wrought-iron chairs, her long legs crossed and her feet resting on the waist-high balcony railing. She seemed completely unconcerned about losing her slip-on sandal, as she tapped her toe against the air in some unheard rhythm. The heel of the shoe swung against her bare foot as it dangled ten stories above Peachtree Street.

Troy followed every swing of her foot, nearly spotlighted in the sunlight. Her open sandals revealed bright red-polished toenails and a splotch of color—a tattoo—just above her right ankle. *Definitely not here on business.*

He continued to stare. Her legs, completely bare, went on forever. And ever. Troy swallowed hard as he studied the smooth skin of her calf, the slimness of her pale thighs. Her tiny jean shorts interrupted his visual assessment of her legs. His gaze skimmed past them to the clingy white tank top she wore, which hugged a generously curved chest.

His heart skipped a beat.

Then he saw her face, complete with full lips and a pert nose. Long lashes rested on her cheeks since her eyes were closed. And her thick mass of auburn hair caught the sunlight and shone like red-hot flames.

Seeing her lips move, and her head nodding in rhythm with her tapping foot, he leaned closer to the door. Even through the glass, he could make out the words she was singing.

"B-b-b-b-ba-ad. I'm bad to the bone."

The sudden rush of familiar heat as his libido returned in full force brought a smile to Troy's lips. Reaching for the handle of the door, he nearly sighed in relief. He hadn't felt this good for a long time. Three months, to be exact.

"Thank you, God," he whispered.

Now it was time to meet the woman who'd so effortlessly awakened him from his long, sexless sleep.

2

"HELLO, ATLANTA. Scarlett has come to pay a visit," Venus Messina murmured to the sky as she reclined on the balcony of the high-rise office building. "Aunt Pitty, hide the silver. And Rhett, if you're out there, call me, baby."

She closed her eyes, thinking she could almost fall asleep in this bright patch of sunlight. Considering the whirlwind of her life over the past seventy-two hours, she supposed it wasn't surprising. She hadn't gotten much sleep lately.

If anyone had suggested last week that within days she'd be in another state, preparing to meet a man who may or may not be her grandfather, she'd have laughed in his face. Or, more likely, cut him off, taken his keys and called a cab.

Yet here she was.

Leaving had been remarkably easy. Joe had insisted he could do without her at Flanagan's. She'd also arranged for her best friend, Lacey, to look after her spoiled cat and her half-dead houseplants. The cat she wanted to come home to. The plants she didn't really care about—but Venus didn't like to admit defeat, and if those dumb ferns were going to die, they would do it at her hand. Lacey would probably have them all healthy and blooming by the time she got back, anyway, just the way she had when she'd lived next door to Venus in their Baltimore apartment complex.

Venus had missed her friend since she'd moved out a year ago. If Lacey were still her neighbor, she probably would have gotten Venus to spill the truth about this trip. Since Lacey was a newlywed, though, it hadn't been hard to keep her in the dark. Lacey was easily distracted by any question about her much-adored spouse, Nate.

Venus wiggled in her chair slightly, the wrought iron hard against her backside. "Pool boy, bring me a frou-frou drink and a more comfortable chaise lounge," she whispered with a grin.

A beach vacation would have been nice. But she had a feeling she was going to like Atlanta, especially with the way things had been going in Baltimore.

She hadn't had a second thought when she'd deposited Leo Gallagher's five-thousand-dollar check, nor when she'd taken a cab to the airport and boarded a plane heading south this morning. Venus still hadn't figured Mr. Gallagher out yet. Either he was one heck of a nice nephew who really wanted to see his uncle happy...which she doubted. Or he was running some kind of scam...which seemed more likely. What her part in the scheme was, she really couldn't say. And for five grand—which would go a long way toward rent, not to mention summer clothes for the foster kids back in Jersey—she wasn't asking many questions.

After all, she wasn't doing anything illegal. She'd simply agreed to visit this Longotti guy for one week, to explore the possibility that she was his long-lost granddaughter. Just because she personally had serious doubts that she was—and didn't particularly *want* to be—did not mean it was entirely impossible. The odds were better than, say, getting struck by lightning. Or winning the lottery.

Or finding a nice guy who wanted to get married and

have a house in the suburbs and a few babies before Venus was too old to enjoy them. She sighed at that cheery thought.

Anyway, whatever Gallagher was up to was on his head, not hers. She was just along for the ride. A well-paid ride.

She had, however, been curious enough to call her foster mother and ask her about the birth certificate. Maureen had told her she'd lost the original in the break-in, but had also said the Child Welfare Agency had forwarded a box of things after Venus had turned eighteen. Confirming she still had the box somewhere, she told Venus she'd mail it to her in Baltimore.

Nearly purring in the warmth of the sun, Venus began to hum, then to sing, a favorite old rock-and-roll song that fit her mood perfectly. When she heard the soft slide of a glass door opening, however, she stopped singing and opened her eyes. She expected to see Leo, accompanied by an old man.

She was almost afraid to look. Would his face seem familiar? Would his smile look like her own? Would he see something in her that reminded him of his long-lost son?

Stop it, Venus. It's not true and you know it.

When she saw a younger man standing there instead, her heart raced faster, anyway.

Good lord, they grew men well in the south!

Shading her eyes with her hand, she studied the stranger in the gray suit. A guy in a tie. Her first impulse should have been to leap off the balcony in self-preservation. But somehow, after months of relative apathy when it came to men, Venus remembered what she so very much liked about them.

Just about everything.

Besides, she was in Atlanta for one week only. How

much damage could even a guy in a tie do in one little week?

First things first—was he tall enough to meet her number-one requirement on her man list? At just a smidge under six feet herself, Venus never went for guys she'd tower over in spike-heeled do-me shoes. A girl had to have her priorities.

All lean, muscled male wrapped up in an elegantly tailored package, this man obviously stood a few inches over six feet tall. *Meets height requirement. Check.*

He was also dark-haired, another personal preference. His thick, chestnut-brown hair was cut conservatively, but ruffled a bit in the strong breeze blowing between the high-rise buildings. It would probably be tousled like that when he woke up in the morning.

Her mouth went dry. She swallowed and continued staring.

His face was magazine-model handsome. Lean jaw, straight, strong nose. Heavily lashed to-die-for eyes the color of springtime leaves. And one of the most kissable mouths she'd ever seen on a guy.

Kissing was one of her personal favorite things to do, and got her vote for being the all-around best activity for the mouth. It ranked even higher than eating rich, dark chocolate, which was probably in her top five. As for the rest of the list...well, that was flexible, depending on her mood, the time of the month and her romantic status. With someone like this incredible man, however, she could definitely picture the possibilities. She nearly moaned at the image.

Her gaze moved lower, to his left hand. *No ring.*

Perfect.

"Good afternoon," she said lazily, her mouth widening in welcome, a signal no man alive could miss.

He smiled back just as lazily, just as aware. Those eyes darkened and his smile faded as they stared at each other for a long, heady moment. Then, taking his cue from her, he expressed not a hint of surprise about finding a strange, casually dressed woman sunning herself out here on the balcony. "Good afternoon to you. Enjoying the sunshine?"

She nodded and turned her face to the sky, drawing in a deep breath. "Love it."

"Be careful," he warned as he sat on the other chair. "It's deceptive with the breeze. Redheads tend to burn, right?"

She raised a brow. "Who says I'm a natural redhead?" At this point in her life, Venus could barely remember what her natural hair color was anymore, though she thought this was pretty close. She'd run the full color spectrum in the past several years. But red was definitely her favorite.

"Whether you are or not, stick with this," he murmured, glancing at her hair with a look so intimate it felt like a touch. "A woman with eyes as green as yours *should* be a redhead."

His quiet flattery hit home. The man was a charmer.

"And a man with a face like yours is usually wearing a wedding ring," she murmured, needing to make sure he was available before they went any further. Venus might like men, but she never went after the taken ones.

"Not married. Not involved," he replied easily.

She wondered if he heard her audible sigh of relief.

When he didn't respond by asking the same question, Venus paused. Was he not interested? Or was he *so* interested he simply didn't give a damn whether she was available or not? Hoping it was the latter, she offered the information anyway. "Me, neither."

Far below them, the traffic rumbled by, evidence of the bustling city life during a hectic Monday rush hour. But up here, high above it all, Venus felt completely separated. Alone. Except for this sexy stranger with the mouth she felt she had to soon kiss or die trying.

He gestured toward her sandal. "That could probably kill someone if it fell from this height."

She intentionally flipped it harder, setting a tapping rhythm with the shoe.

He grinned. "Okay, so I've got ulterior motives for wanting you to move your legs." He leaned forward, resting his elbows on his knees, and stared intently at her foot. "What is it?"

"I think it's called a shoe."

He chuckled. "No, I meant *that*." He pointed toward her ankle. Leaning even closer, he reached for her leg and gently tugged her foot off the railing. Venus sucked in a breath at the feel of his warm fingers on her calf, wondering if he heard the crazy pounding of her heart within her chest. She heard it—it roared to life in her head as she focused every bit of her attention on the brush of his skin against hers.

"This," he said softly as he placed her foot on his knee, completely disregarding any possible damage to his expensive trousers. Then he leaned over to look at her tattoo. He touched the tiny hummingbird she'd had put on as an unemployment present last year. "Very pretty. Did it hurt?"

She could only manage to shake her head. If she tried to make a sound, it would emerge as a whimper. Or a plea.

He continued touching her, tracing the shape of the blue-green bird with the tip of his finger, cupping the back of her calf with his other hand.

The chair suddenly felt harder against her bottom. She shifted uncomfortably in the suddenly too-tight jean shorts. And her breath barely made it into her lungs as she focused on the way he looked at her. The way he touched her.

"Why a hummingbird?" he asked, still not letting go.

She didn't answer at first, not quite able to. She couldn't even think of anything but the way his gentle touch would feel, sliding up her leg, beneath her shorts. Touching her where she suddenly felt hot and achy.

Finally, drawing in a ragged breath, she whispered, "I like hummingbirds. They're aggressive as hell, but still delicate and small. Just like I always wanted to be."

Shaking his head reprovingly, he tsked. "Why do women always want to be the opposite of what they are? Even when they're stunningly beautiful?"

She snorted a laugh, drawing his stare to her face. Okay, she *was* the opposite of delicate and small. But she didn't think she was the opposite of aggressive. Or so she'd been told. Then she focused on the stunningly beautiful part.

That worked.

"I've suddenly discovered I really like tall women."

Oh, yay!

"Any other tattoos anywhere?" he asked, letting his gaze travel across her bare shoulders and neck.

Her body reacted, her nipples hardening beneath her shirt. Feeling them scrape against the cotton, she wondered if he noticed. "No," she said. "But I'm thinking about it. I'm not sure I'll like my next choice once I turn seventy-five or eighty."

He raised a questioning brow. "Next choice?"

She nodded. "Jessica Rabbit."

When no look of understanding crossed his face, Venus gestured toward her top. If he hadn't seen her body's reaction to the way he'd held her foot before, he'd surely notice it now.

She tugged the cotton tight, revealing the sexy, red-haired cartoon character vamping it up on the front of her T-shirt. In a bubble above the bombshell's head were the words, "I'm not bad. I'm just drawn that way."

Venus liked the sentiment.

"Ahh," he said, staring hard at her shirt. His voice sounded thick. Yeah, he'd noticed.

"She doesn't look like a rabbit," he offered, still delicately stroking her ankle, absently caressing her calf until she nearly writhed in her chair.

"She's, uh, not..." Venus managed to reply. "That's her married name."

"What about you? Are you bad? Or are you just drawn that way?"

She closed her eyes, leaning back in her seat, silently asking him to continue the tender stroking of her leg. "Maybe I'll let you figure it out for yourself," she murmured.

He finally let go of her foot, as if realizing they were moving *really* fast for a couple of people who hadn't yet introduced themselves.

"I've thought about getting one," he admitted, gently shifting her foot off his lap. Then he chuckled ruefully. "Not that anyone would believe it."

"Why not?"

He answered with a secretive smile. "Let's just say people see me in a certain way. A tattoo wouldn't go with the image."

"I know how that goes," she muttered, not even able to count the times someone had been surprised by her intelligence, or the business sense hidden beneath the exterior package and smart mouth. "But you don't exactly look like Mister Boring Businessman." Gesturing toward his tanned skin, she mused, "Looks like you're no stranger to the sun yourself."

"I actually live on the beach in south Florida. Or rather, I did, until last week."

"You moved here? To Atlanta?"

"Not permanently. I'm not sure where I'll end up. I've recently found myself with a lot more freedom than I expected."

She couldn't resist. "So you made parole, huh?"

Deadpan, he nodded. "Certainly. Amazing how quickly they let us homicidal maniacs out nowadays."

"Tell me you didn't get sent up the river for throwing red-haired females over balconies."

He shook his head, a twinkle in his pale green eyes. "Only natural redheads."

She gave an exaggerated sigh of relief. "Whew."

"So," he continued. "Should I ask who you are and what you're doing here? Or should we just leave now and go straight to...dinner?"

She liked his directness. And she suspected his pause had been quite deliberate. They'd exchanged only a few dozen sentences, but she'd mentally substituted another word for "dinner," and she'd bet he had too. As surely as she'd bet that word was "bed."

Venus, you swore off men, remember? Even before this whole long-lost granddaughter business.

Somehow, she couldn't bring herself to care. The instant chemistry between her and the stranger was something she hadn't experienced before. Ever.

Sure, she'd had her fair share of relationships with men. Probably enough fair shares for two or three women, if she wanted to be completely honest about it.

That had been part of the reason she'd decided to take a break from them after losing her job.

Other reasons had probably included Lacey's blissfully happy marriage. Plus Venus's brief fling with Raul, a hunky young guy who worked with Lacey. She'd dated Raul in the brief period between dumping Dale, the loser at work, and getting paid back by him with the loss of her job.

Raul, though a good bit younger than she, had been a doll, and she'd found herself caring about him quite a lot. If he'd been older, and at a different place in his life, Venus could have fallen in love with him. But they were moving in different directions and realized they worked best as friends.

Still, having pictured love, she almost found herself wanting it. True love, marriage, the whole she-bang...with the right person. Eventually. After she'd gotten over what dickhead Dale had done to her.

Eight months seemed just about long enough to get over backstabbing and betrayal. Besides, she'd missed some parts of her former lifestyle. Particularly men. Venus liked men. She liked dating. Liked going out dancing, or to ball games, or just for walks at the Inner Harbor back home in Baltimore.

And she liked sex. Really liked it. *So sue me.*

As much as she'd enjoyed getting to know men—usually the wrong ones—she'd never felt such an instant, sudden, overwhelming desire for one. Especially not while stone-cold sober. So she at least ought to find out his name.

"My name's Venus," she said. She scooted her chair closer until her bare knees nearly touched his blue trousers.

"How appropriate," he murmured.

"I think so. You would be..."

"Troy."

"How nice to meet you, Troy. I'd love to go to *dinner* with you, but unfortunately tonight's not possible." She gestured toward his tasteful necktie and gave him a flirtatious grin. "Besides, I've recently sworn off guys in ties."

He shrugged. "Easily remedied. I'll take it off."

"And suits," she said, knowing he could hear a suggestive purr in her voice.

"It can come off too." His tone was just as suggestive.

She raised a wicked brow and glanced at the other buildings nearby. "Hmm, that could be interesting. But aren't you worried some of these executives in their cubbyholes keep binoculars around? I know I would if you were in the habit of standing out here, taking off your...tie."

He laughed out loud, a warm, rich laugh that rolled over her body and made her tingle. She liked the sound of it as much as she liked the curve of his lips.

Taking a deep breath, she suddenly wondered what other interesting sounds the man was capable of. Sighs. Moans. Shouts.

She nearly shuddered at the thought.

"I didn't mean here," he said.

She pouted. "Aww, gee."

"Tomorrow?" he asked. "I promise not to overdress."

Or dress at all? Oh, yes, the man knew how to play this game. But before she could go any further, she needed to find out just who he was. "So, are you here today for a meeting or something?" she asked, hearing a hopeful note in her own voice. *Please say yes.* She hoped like crazy that he didn't work here, in the suite of offices used by Max Longotti's catalog company, Longotti Lines. Because she really didn't want to start off her relationship with her supposed/could-be/maybe grandfather by seducing one of his employees.

Not that she'd have to do the seducing. If she was any judge—and she *was*—the man looked fully capable of seduction. She shivered slightly, in spite of the heat of the brightly lit afternoon.

"Actually, that's my office." He pointed over his shoulder to the door through which he'd emerged moments before.

Moments? Had she really discovered the existence of this man who made her heart pound like crazy and her legs feel weak and boneless mere moments before?

She finally thought about his reply and her heart sank, along with her plans. "Your office. Right there. So, uh, you work here? For Max Longotti?" When he nodded, she tried to contain a disappointed sigh.

"I'm Max's new V.P. For now," he continued.

Perfect. Just perfect. She'd met a man who'd finally made her rethink her "men aren't worth the trouble" stance, and she couldn't have him. It simply would not be smart to get involved with this man, no matter how delicious he was.

Leo would not be happy if she did what she really wanted to do with this handsome, charming stranger. He seemed intent on "pleasing" his uncle by presenting him with his sweet and lovely long-lost grandchild.

Sweet she wasn't, which is exactly what she'd told Leo. So he'd settled for bright and lovely. Still, he had insisted that she be as discreet as possible, and she'd agreed.

And even Venus—who'd been called everything in her life, *except* discreet—knew sleeping with Max's executive might not be the height of discretion.

As a matter of fact, the guy would have to be completely off-limits. Starting right now.

Hell.

TROY SENSED IT the moment the stunning redhead began to withdraw. Her smile faded, her eyelashes lowered and she turned away in her chair to stare at the skyline. Because he worked here? Interesting...

"Now, why don't you tell me who are you, and why you're here, Venus?"

"I'm just visiting."

Her voice was cool, when it had previously been warm. That didn't concern him. The heat in her eyes two minutes ago could have melted solid ice. "From where?"

"Baltimore."

She swung her feet up on the rail again, silently dismissing him. Troy almost laughed, seeing through the maneuver. He paused to appreciate again those long-enough-to-wrap-around-him-twice legs and had to shift in his seat.

No. The cold shoulder wasn't going to change the way they'd reacted to one another from the start. Or the way he was reacting to her now.

If she worked for Max and was worried about a no-fraternization policy, he might just have to quit his new job. It was a small enough sacrifice. What job could compare to getting his libido back?

"Have you been to Atlanta before?"

She merely shook her head.

Getting answers from her was like pulling teeth, but Troy was not about to give up. Not now that he'd met her, now that he'd seen those beautiful green eyes of hers up close, caught a whiff of her exotic perfume and heard the husky timbre of her voice. He could still feel the smoothness of her skin on the tips of his sensitized fingers.

He wanted her, not knowing who she was or why she was here. And she wanted him too.

It was just that simple.

"What do you do?"

She glanced at him out of the corner of her eye and said, "Right now, I'm a bartender."

He nearly chuckled until he realized she was serious. Then he shrugged. "Remind me never to offer to make you a drink."

"I don't imagine you'd ever have reason to," she replied firmly. "I'll only be in town for a week."

Ouch. A definite rebuff. But Troy hadn't earned his reputation by being easily rebuffed. "Where are you staying?"

"At the Longotti estate." Then, she grudgingly added, "At least, I *think* so. I'm supposed to go over there this afternoon."

He hid a grin. Max hadn't mentioned another houseguest. He could hardly wait to bump into her coming out of the shower or knock on her door at night to borrow some toothpaste.

He wondered if she slept naked. Then he wondered just how long it would take him to find out. Not long, he hoped.

It was too bad he'd be moving out in a few days. Then again, maybe his new apartment wouldn't be ready for a week. Maybe he'd make damn sure it wasn't. "So, why aren't you sure you're staying with Max? He knows you're coming, doesn't he?"

As she nibbled her full lower lip, the heat in his gut shot up another notch. She had a mouth made for kissing. And other things.

"Not exactly," she mumbled. "Leo dropped me off here, then went to find him. He's, uh, setting things up, I think."

"Leo? Leo Gallagher, Max's nephew?"

She nodded.

Not good. Leo was a white-haired weasel, as far as Troy could tell. Not that it was his place to judge, of course. He barely knew the man, who had some high-level job in this company, though no one seemed sure exactly what he did. But he did know Max's nephew had been vehemently opposed to Troy's arrival, and to the possibility of the company being sold.

Apparently, from what Max said, Leo had fully imagined himself to be heir apparent and had been angling for more than a decade for Max to retire so he could step in. Max referred to him as the pencil-necked leech and said he'd retire when they pried his office keys out of his cold dead hand. Or when he passed them over to a new owner—which somehow made Troy think Leo's job aspirations weren't going to pan out.

Venus must have noticed his sudden silence, and his frown. "You know Leo?" she asked.

"Barely."

"You barely know him, but you know you don't like him?"

He hedged. "I don't *dislike* him, I only met him last week when I started working for Longotti Lines."

Her eyes widened and she finally turned to give him her full attention again. "You just started your job? I thought maybe you'd just gotten a promotion and transferred in from Florida or something."

"Today is my one-week anniversary." Leaning closer, he went for smooth charm, since honest conversation hadn't gotten her to relax, the way she had at first. "I never imagined perks like beautiful redheads sunning themselves right outside my door when I took the job. Maybe I should stock up on sunscreen. Would you like me to do your back?"

She rolled her eyes. "Save it. I liked you better when you weren't being oily. Besides, you're not very good at it."

He straightened, not sure whether he felt amused or offended. Then a reluctant chuckle crossed his lips. "All right, Venus. In the interest of being strictly sincere, I personally think Leo Gallagher is a shifty, spoiled man with abominable taste in shoes and a need for a good barber."

She grinned. "My, my, from oily to pompous. You are a contradiction, aren't you?"

Pompous? She'd just called him *pompous?* He raised a brow and leaned closer. "You're one to talk about contradictions. From sultress to iceberg in under a minute."

He stared into her brilliant green eyes, daring her to disagree. She didn't even try. "It's a woman's prerogative to change her mind."

"So you don't want to have dinner with me?" He dared her to deny it, knowing damn well she did.

She raised a skeptical brow. "Oh, you mean we were really talking about dinner?"

"What else could we have been talking about?"

"I was thinking more along the lines of dessert." Her voice held a note of challenge.

"I hadn't even asked about dessert," he said, his voice holding a hint of playful challenge.

Her creamy cheeks began to grow pink with obvious embarrassment. He doubted this woman blushed very often and he found the heightened color in her face extremely attractive.

He let her sweat for a moment. Then, unable to lie to

her any more than he could to himself, he said, "But I would have."

Her answer was equally as honest. "Five minutes ago the answer probably would have been yes."

"And now?"

"Now it's got to be no."

"Why?"

She merely shook her head, unable or unwilling to answer. Troy, however, wasn't one to give up without a fight. "Can you give me one chance to change your mind?"

She eyed him warily but didn't refuse. Letting her see his small confident smile, he leaned closer, catching her exotic scent. Then closer, until he saw the pulse beating wildly in her neck. And closer still, until their lips were a breath apart.

"You think you can change my mind with a kiss?" she whispered.

He responded with a slow nod and a lazy drawl. "Yes."

She visibly stiffened at the certainty in his tone.

"You think I can't?"

She responded to his challenge with a raised eyebrow and a taunting look. "You can try."

He did, slipping his fingers into her hair, tangling his hands in that thick mass of living fire. He touched his lips to hers, gently at first, tasting her, savoring the softness of her mouth. Only when she moaned low in her throat did he go farther, sliding his tongue between his lips, letting it mate lazily with hers in a hot, intoxicating dance that sent intense sensations rushing through his body.

She tasted sweet and ripe, like summer fruit. But warm, like fine whiskey. She moaned again and tilted her head, kissing him back just as deliberately, just as invitingly.

He tugged her closer, until, somehow, she was sitting on his lap, her arms wrapped around his neck, his around her jean-clad hips. He skimmed his fingers beneath her cotton top. Lightly touching the bare flesh at her waist, he heard her sigh against his kiss as skin met skin.

Finally, he moved his mouth from hers, kissing the corner of her lips, then her cheek. Her jaw. Her neck.

"Changed your mind yet?" he growled against her throat.

"Uh-huh," she whispered.

"Good. Tell me what time we can get together tomorrow night." He scraped his teeth along her collarbone, feeling the way she jerked against him in response. "If you're *sure* tonight's out, that is."

She groaned in frustration. "It's definitely out."

Before he could attempt to cajole her, she pulled back. "I think I hear voices."

She was up, off his lap, standing at the rail so fast, he thought he'd imagined their heated kiss.

"Are you sure? I don't hear anything," he said, wanting her back in his arms. Immediately, if not sooner. He stood and joined her at the railing.

Before she could answer, a sliding glass door opened behind them. Max stepped out, followed by his nephew, Leo. Max looked tense, appearing very much the seventy-four-year-old man he was. Leo, on the other hand, looked positively euphoric.

Max glanced briefly at Troy, dismissed him, then focused on Venus. "Is this true?"

She stood up straighter. Beside her, Troy could easily see the way her hands trembled, until she clenched them together in front of her. Her mouth opened, but she didn't speak.

"Is what true?" Troy asked.

"Of course it is," Leo said.

Max ignored them both and stepped closer to Venus. "Is it possible? Is it really you...Violet?"

Confused, Troy said, "Her name's..."

"Yes, I told you, I'm certain it's true," Leo interjected, stepping between Troy and Max. He took Venus's hand and pulled her forward, looking as happy as a kid with a surprise cereal box toy. "Uncle Max, meet your long-lost granddaughter."

3

OF COURSE? CERTAIN? TRUE?

Venus wanted to strangle Leo Gallagher. So much for his assurances that this would just be a "visit" to see if it was "possible" she could be the person he claimed she was. He'd obviously presented it to the old man as a done deal.

Well, it wasn't a done deal, not in her book. Five grand or no five grand, she'd never agreed to outright lie.

"Actually, my name's Venus," she said, hearing an edge in her own voice. She shot Leo an angry look before turning her full attention to Max Longotti. "Venus Messina."

The old man, with a thick head of brilliant white hair and piercing gray eyes, met her unflinching stare. "Messina. I see. How old are you, Ms. Messina?"

"That's a nice way to start a conversation with a woman," she tossed off, still annoyed at being manipulated. "You gonna ask me my bra size next?"

Out of the corner of her eye, she saw Leo wince, then draw his brow into a frown. He'd warned her to be discreet.

Not a good start. Especially since if it weren't for her really keen sense of hearing, she would have been caught making out with the hired help three minutes ago.

"I'm not so old that I can't make a fair guess at that," the old gentleman said, his tone droll and amused.

Venus chuckled. Score one for Grandpa.

Beside Leo, Troy watched silently. He leaned casually against the balcony railing, arms crossed in front of his chest, absorbing every word they said. The bright sunlight cast bits of gold on his dark brown hair, and she was again struck by the sheer handsomeness of the man. Amazing to look at, and hands down the best kisser she'd ever known. Her lips and tongue still tingled.

As if he read her thoughts, he met her eye and smiled slightly. *We have a secret, don't we?* his smile seemed to say.

She wondered what he must think of this whole thing. It seemed like science fiction even to her.

"Now," Max Longotti continued softly, "will you *please* tell me exactly when you were born, young lady?"

She rattled off her birth date, hating to admit being almost thirty in front of Troy. Not that it mattered, she reminded herself. Before that unreal kiss, she'd decided he was off-limits. And after it, well, he'd still be off-limits...after she got at least one more kiss from the man...or two...or...

Max nodded. "And you say your father was actually my son?"

"I didn't say jack," she retorted, dragging her attention away from the hottie with the intense look on his face. "Since I never laid eyes on my father, he coulda been Jimmy Hoffa for all I know." She gestured toward Leo. "But your nephew here seems to think it's possible."

Leo's subsequent frown would have scared small children.

"Maybe I should excuse myself," Troy finally said. "This appears to be a family matter."

"Yes," Leo began.

"No," Max Longotti insisted. "An outsider's viewpoint might be useful here." He turned back to Venus. "I know what my nephew thinks. I want to know what *you* think, Ms. Messina."

Sensing her answer was very important to the man, who suddenly appeared a little less strong and sure than he had at first, she admitted, "I suppose it's *possible*. Stranger things have happened. I mean, who'd have ever thought fat-free potato chips would actually *not* taste like cardboard?"

She saw Troy's lips curve slightly.

"But you personally don't think it's true. You don't believe my nephew's claims," the old man prodded.

Leo touched his uncle's arm. "Max, the evidence..."

Max ignored him. "What happened to your mother?"

"She died when I was eight."

"Then who raised you?"

"I was lucky enough to be placed in a really good foster home. My foster mother raised me until I left home at eighteen."

"Your mother had no family?"

Venus shrugged. "None who wanted *me*."

She didn't glance at Troy, not wanting to see a look of pity on his face. She'd never pitied herself, and she'd damn sure never wanted it from anybody else. Especially not a man with whom she was in serious lust.

"So, judging by your birth date, it is very likely you were conceived during the weeks my son spent in New York. If he was, indeed, your father, your parents' relationship would have to have been a very...brief one."

She tensed, waiting for him to make one crack about her mother's morals. Venus might not know much about her biological father, but she'd adored her always-smiling mother until Trina had drawn her last breath. If this stranger spoke one negative word about her, Venus would be out the door so fast he'd think she'd fallen off the balcony.

He didn't. "So it is possible that your mother never knew my son by any other name than the one he adopted for the stage."

"There's that word again...possible," Venus said, surprised at the relief flowing through her veins just because the old man hadn't passed judgment on her mother.

He continued softly, talking almost to himself. "And it's also possible she had difficulty reaching him to tell him about you. She must have been desperate." He glanced at the sky, continuing to formulate his theory aloud. "Perhaps she sent your picture, with the name Violet on the back, to a club in Los Angeles. The letter might have had only his stage name on it. It could have taken a long time for it to catch up to him." He returned his gaze to Venus. "But when he did receive it, it changed everything. He was coming back."

"More could haves and might haves," she insisted, knowing the man was speculating. She still couldn't bring herself to believe this scenario. It was too farfetched. Too coincidental.

Too damned heartbreaking.

Venus didn't *want* to believe her father had died within days...maybe hours...of finding out about her. She didn't *want* to think of her mother—who'd said she'd fallen ass over elbows in love with the man when they'd bickered over a cab in the rain—wasting the last eight years of her life waiting for someone who was already long gone. She couldn't bear to think of Trina pining for a man who'd gotten her message, planned to come back to them...and then died before ever being able to do so.

No, the whole thing was too sad. And Venus wasn't into sad.

Feeling moisture in her eyes, she swung around, turning her back to the three men. She stared out at the sky, blinking rapidly, groping for control. Then, she felt a hand on her shoulder, a supportive squeeze, a tender offer of reassurance.

Turning her head, she saw Troy standing there. He didn't say anything, didn't offer trite, nurturing words. He just let her know she wasn't alone, with a small nod and a look of intense concern on his face. She took a deep breath, sucking up his silently offered strength. Then, crossing her arms in front of her chest, she faced Max again. "Let me ask you something now."

He waited expectantly.

"If all this is true—and I think that's a big humongous if—why'd it take almost thirty years to find me?"

Max glanced at Leo. "My nephew apparently thought of something I never did all those years ago. We assumed Max, my son, had been involved with someone in California. We focused our search efforts there. And, of course, we used his real name."

Leo smiled. She thought he was going for self-deprecating, but his expression looked self-congratulatory instead. "I'm so sorry I didn't think of the possibility of him meeting someone in New York long ago. Nor of having a private investigator search birth records in the northeast to see if Max Longotti *or* Matt Messina turned up as a father during that time."

She immediately latched on to his words. "Birth records. So you *have* seen a copy of my birth certificate?"

Leo's jovial expression never faltered. "No, I left it in the hands of the investigator. He is the one who obtained those records, then tracked you down. I simply utilized the address he provided."

Smooth. Reasonable. But she didn't completely buy it.

"Is he going to send you those records?"

A slight narrowing of his eyes indicated his annoyance. "I'm sure I'll receive them now that the case is concluded."

Wanting to gauge the man's reaction, Venus said, "My foster mother said she does have some paperwork, after all. She's digging it out and mailing it to my home in Baltimore."

Leo stared at her for a moment, then his smile thinned. "Good."

Troy, who'd been standing quietly for several moments, cleared his throat.

"You have something to contribute, Troy?" Max asked.

Troy raised a brow. "It seems you're at an impasse," he offered. "You may discuss dates, pseudonyms and birth certificates all afternoon and never come to an agreement."

He sounded like a businessman brokering a big deal. Venus almost rolled her eyes, wondering where the flirty hunk who'd kissed her until she was brainless and limp had gotten to.

"Wouldn't it be simpler to just conduct a DNA test?" he finally concluded.

"I've already thought of that," Leo interjected. He touched his uncle's arm. "Of course, knowing your mistrust of newfangled science, I made sure to contact one of the experts in the field. When I hear back from him, we'll bring him to Atlanta and have him conduct the test."

"Yes, yes, of course," Max agreed. He raised a quivering hand to his brow, looking out of sorts. "Splendid. That's much more conclusive than any birth records, which aren't entirely reliable. DNA. Marvelous thing."

DNA tests? Conclusive proof? Things were going too

fast for Venus's taste. She hadn't decided if she liked this old guy, and she definitely hadn't decided if she even wanted to know the truth!

She cocked her head and raised her hand, wiggling her fingers in a little wave. "Hello? Anybody going to ask *me* if I'm willing to roll up my sleeve and let some stranger poke needles into me? What if I don't particularly like needles?"

"Actually, I think they swab your cheek," Troy explained.

She shot him a glare that told him to mind his own business. "Oh, you've undergone these tests before? Have lots of potential illegitimate junior executives running around out there, do you?"

As he stiffened, Venus cursed her quick temper and sarcasm. Troy had only been trying to help, after all.

Her barb had obviously angered him. His eyes narrowed. "You don't seem very anxious to confirm your claim, Ms. Messina."

"It's not my claim."

"Perhaps not," he admitted. "Or perhaps you *want* Max to think you don't believe it. Throwing your arms around him and calling him Grandpa might have made him suspect your motives. This insistence that you're not may make him more sympathetic." He stepped closer, until the tips of his shoes almost touched her toes. She forced herself to stay still, so close to him she could smell his warm cologne and see the beating of his pulse in his neck. She could think of nothing except the way his mouth had tasted against hers, just minutes before.

"And generous," he finally concluded.

Venus didn't follow at first. She was too focused on her instinctive reaction to him. The heat radiating from his body, the coiled strength concealed beneath the conservative suit. And, unfortunately, the absence of the warm, tender concern that had been in his eyes just minutes before.

"Generous?" she asked, hearing the breathiness in her voice.

"I wonder what your motives were in coming to Atlanta," he said softly, as if merely speculating aloud. "They didn't have anything to do with money, did they?"

Money? He thought she'd come here to try to scam money off the old man? She was about to tell him to take a flying leap off the balcony when she remembered she *had* been paid—and paid well—to take this trip. She swallowed her angry words and lowered her eyes, her whole body stiffening as she acknowledged the partial truth of his accusation. He made a sound that could have been a sigh, then stepped away from her.

"Mr. Longotti," she said, turning her back on the annoyingly handsome man who suddenly had such a low opinion of her, "I'm being straight with you here. I don't think I'm who your nephew says I am. I don't even know if I *want* to be, if you can dig that." She shot a look over her shoulder at Troy, who still watched with suspicion and distrust. "But I am willing to talk to you about it some more. And, perhaps, to consider a test if we *both* decide it's what we want."

The elderly gentleman blinked, then stared at her, his gaze looking sharper and more direct. He seemed to be looking for something in her eyes, a gauge of her honesty, perhaps? Or some reminder of the son he'd lost? Finally he nodded. "Agreed."

"Yes, excellent. These things do take time," Leo murmured, holding his elderly uncle by the arm. "Uncle Max, you look very pale. Perhaps we should go now?"

"I'm fine," he snapped. "I want to visit with my…with Ms. Messina here."

"But your doctor's appointment," Leo continued. "You said you were supposed to see the doctor this afternoon."

"Oh, yes," he murmured. "I'd forgotten. That's what I was planning to do until you almost shocked me into a heart attack with this news." Max frowned at his nephew. "I can reschedule. I want to get her settled in at home."

"I can take Ms. Messina over," Troy interjected. "Max, you go keep your appointment, then head home and meet us there. I think it might be good for everyone to have a little while alone before any further conversation, don't you?"

He shot Venus a look daring her to disagree. Not that she would. She wanted to be alone, to reconsider just what she'd gotten herself into here. Things suddenly didn't seem as simple as they had this morning, when she'd thought she'd take advantage of a paid vacation in the south.

More than ever, she thought Leo Gallagher was up to no good. It looked like he planned to use her for whatever it was he wanted. The way he'd presented her to his uncle—so unlike how they'd agreed—was a clear indication he couldn't be trusted.

For the first time in ages—probably since she'd first been taken into custody by the state, been told that her mother's distant family didn't want her and that she had to go to a foster home—Venus began to feel very alone. In Baltimore, at least, she had friends—Lacey, Uncle Joe and many others. She was completely comfortable in her world, even if that world consisted only of her apartment, her cat and Flanagan's. There were a dozen people there she could call if she needed help…or just a sympathetic ear.

Here, though, she had only three men, three near strangers. Leo, who apparently wanted to use her. Max, who likely wanted her to be someone she was not. And Troy, a man she was incredibly attracted to, but couldn't have. A man whose kiss had made every thought flee her brain and made her body willing to do absolutely anything so long as he kept touching her. A man who, at this moment, wasn't too impressed with her.

That knowledge, more than anything, made her stomach knot and her body tense. She had a sinking feeling Troy was going to be the most difficult situation of all.

TROY WAS GLAD to get Max Longotti and his undoubtedly scheming nephew out the door. He wanted to be alone with Ms. Venus Messina, or whatever her name was. He had a few things to say to her. A few things to get straight.

The woman was easy to read, almost an open book. She wore her feelings on her face, and was obviously ruled by her emotions, as many passionate people were. As an observer, a thinker, Troy had long ago learned to pay attention to other people's expressions and body language. He gauged reactions of others before deciding on his own actions.

Hers—when he'd confronted her about the issue of money—had been damning. Troy couldn't shake the strong feeling of disappointment he'd felt when he'd seen a flash of guilt in her eyes. She hadn't been able to meet his stare for more than ten seconds. Her shoulders had stiffened and her lush bottom lip had disappeared as she sucked it into her mouth in dismay.

Yes, money definitely had something to do with Venus being in Atlanta.

And no matter how much he wanted to take her in his arms and kiss her again, he knew he couldn't do it. Maybe the old Troy wouldn't have given a damn if he'd gone to bed with a thief or a liar. This Troy did. As much as he wanted her—*really* wanted her—he wasn't going anywhere near the redhead until he figured out what the hell she was up to.

Troy remained silent as they exited the building. Good manners dictated that he hold the door for her, and the sight of her folding her long legs into his low-slung sports car hit him in the gut with the intensity of a punch. Five more minutes on that balcony and he might have felt those legs wrapped around him.

Enough. More than likely, the woman was a con artist. Or else she was Max Longotti's grandchild. Either way, she was off-limits. If she was Max's granddaughter, having a hot affair with her would likely ruin his relationship with his new boss.

If she was up to no good with Max's nephew, they could hurt the old man, whom Troy had grown to care about. Max reminded him of his own grandmother, Sophie, whose strict, controlled exterior hid someone fiercely loyal to family. Unlike Sophie, Max had no close family. With the exception of Leo, a few assorted cousins, and now this mysterious redhead, he had no one.

Given Leo's attitude since Troy's arrival in Atlanta, any plan would probably also involve the company. Meaning it involved Troy directly. He liked Longotti Lines and saw tremendous potential for a merger or an outright sale to his family.

Troy had been paying careful attention to a major merger that had taken place last year between a national retail chain and a popular outfitter catalog company. This current deal could have the same result, each firm benefiting by tapping into the other's strengths. Longotti Lines was known for its southern-themed products for the tasteful home, but had all the standard problems with distribution and marketing as any mail-order business. Langtree's was quickly becoming renowned as an upper-crust department store in south Florida, but wasn't as far-reaching as it should be due to its geographic limitations.

A merger could be a perfect marriage. It could also be the perfect opportunity for Troy to bring something new and fresh to the Langtree family business. Since his father had returned to manage the stores, Troy wanted something of his own, something to take on and make successful. It wasn't that anybody in his family expected him to prove anything to them, and he didn't feel the need to. This was more a matter of proving something to *himself*.

He wanted this catalog acquisition to happen. And he wanted to make it a triumphant success for both companies. Because if he didn't, he honestly didn't know what he would do with his career.

After pulling out of the parking lot of the office building, he kept his eyes on the road, not on the sexy legs of the woman in the passenger seat. He had no intention of getting into an argument with her here in the close confines of his car. Hell, just the warm smell of her musky cologne was enough of a distraction—he didn't want to kill them both in a wreck. They would have time to talk when they got back to Max's estate up in Buckhead.

She, apparently, had no such reservations. "You've got a fat lot of nerve, mister," she snapped.

He shot her a look out the corner of his eye. She was turned in the seat, facing him, arms crossed and steam practically coming out of her ears. "I beg your pardon?"

"You think I'm a con artist, don't you?"

Focused on navigating the traffic-filled street, he shrugged. "I didn't say that."

"You didn't have to. Your attitude said it. You think I'm up to something, just because I'm not falling all over myself to get tests to prove I'm related to someone I haven't even decided I *want* to be related to."

"A very wealthy someone," he replied easily, not allowing her to bait him into raising his voice.

"All the more reason for me to not want to be here. Do you think I don't know how out of place I am with the Max Longotti types? You think I intentionally want to throw myself to a pack of rich wolves who'd tear me apart because I don't know a salad fork from a dessert fork?"

"They're interchangeable, unless they have distinct triangular points at the ends of the outmost tines," he explained, not even thinking about it. "Then it's a salad fork."

Silence. He glanced at her, seeing her staring at him as if he had two heads. "Gag me," she finally muttered.

Troy bit his lip to hide a grin, entertained again by her forthright personality. He couldn't make sense of the woman, who outwardly appeared very open and sometimes shockingly honest. That just didn't gel with the image of a deceptive con artist.

They rode in silence for a few minutes. Then, stopping at a traffic signal, he finally turned to meet her stare, forcing himself to focus on what she was up to, not the way she looked—not the pale curve of her cheek, the fullness of her lips or that tantalizing hollow in her throat.

He stiffened, mentally ordering his body to stop reacting to her when his mind didn't trust her one bit. "You must admit, money is a large motivation for a lot of things, Ms. Messina."

She held his eye, not turning away or blushing. "I'm not after Max Longotti's money, Mr....Vice President!"

Her reaction was different than when the money issue had come up before. So either he'd misread her earlier, or else she'd better prepared herself to answer the question. He honestly couldn't say which he believed more. "My last name is Langtree."

She snorted. "Figures."

He was almost afraid to ask. "Why?"

"Because it sounds rich and uptight. Like you."

"I didn't seem too uptight for you up on that balcony when we met," he said softly, daring her to disagree.

"No, then you were oily and pompous."

He couldn't prevent a small laugh from spilling across his lips. The woman was damned stubborn and fiery as hell. Surprisingly, he found himself liking the combination, even when she was hurling insults at his head. "So," he asked, "which was I when we kissed? Uptight, oily or pompous?"

She didn't say anything at first, and Troy almost regretted baiting her. Neither of them needed to be reminded of the sexy conversation they'd shared on the balcony, nor of their erotic kiss. Had the circumstances been different, they may very well have been driving to a hotel right now. And they both knew it.

He could almost hear her breaths deepening in spite of the sounds of traffic and the purr of his car's engine. A quick look confirmed her sudden confusion—obviously she was thinking of that sultry, electric connection they'd felt from the first moment. Her eyes were wide, her lips parted. Seeing the tightness of her nipples under her clingy cotton shirt, Troy suddenly felt hot in spite of the steady stream of cool air emerging from the car vents. He remembered how her breasts had felt against his chest, the way his mouth had hungered for them. His body hummed as he reexperienced the way she tasted, the softness of her skin. He shifted in his seat, willing himself to forget her deep, seductive laugh, and the way the sun turned her long hair into living, red-hot flames.

Off-limits or not, con woman or heiress, she still attracted him like no one had in a very long time. "Cat got your tongue, Ms. Messina? Just whose lap do you think you were sitting on less than an hour ago?" he finally said, almost regretting the suggestiveness of the words as soon as they left his mouth.

"A body double," she finally mumbled.

Considering he was an identical twin, that amused him. "My body double wouldn't have asked at all. Trent tends to go for what he wants without thinking about it first."

She edged closer to her door, giving him a wary look. "Do you have a split personality? Like that guy in *Psycho*?"

He laughed again. "No, just a twin. He lives in Florida."

"Oh, great, two of you. Is he quick to judge, like you?"

Quick to judge? That's what she thought of him? The accusation was almost funny, considering how he and Trent always viewed one another. Trent leapt without looking. Troy viewed a situation from every angle before deciding on a course of action. "We're not much alike," he admitted, "other than physically. What about you? I take it you have no siblings?"

"No biological ones. I stay in touch with some of the other foster kids I grew up with. And my foster mom has four great kids right now who think of me as a big sister. I get back to see them as much as I can."

The note of affection in her voice couldn't have been feigned. She made no attempt to hide her background, seemed completely accepting and comfortable with the way she'd been raised—another detail that didn't quite gel with the image of her as a clever con woman. "So, you say you don't want money. Why don't you tell me what it is you're really after?"

"I'm not after anything. Leo asked me to come, to meet Max and consider the possibility of us being related." She turned in her seat, facing forward and shaking her head. Her voice dropped to a whisper. "It sounded simple."

"A simple con?"

She groaned in frustration. "*Not* a con. At least not by me. Leo made it sound like it could be true, and I owed it to myself, and Max, to check it out."

He raised a brow. "Checking it out. Yes, that would certainly explain the big reunion scene, culminating with the introduction of the long-lost granddaughter."

"You really can be a snot, can't you?" she snapped back.

Though he'd just changed lanes in heavy traffic, Troy couldn't help jerking his head to look at her. "Did you just call me a snot?"

She answered only with a smirk.

As he had from the moment he'd met her, Troy felt completely unsure how to react. The woman was outrageous and confident. Brazen and funny. Cocky with moments of vulnerability. A complete contradiction. She confused him. She aroused him. She angered him. He'd never met anyone like her. He still wanted her so much it nearly caused him physical pain.

As if completely oblivious to his reaction, Venus

reached for the stereo and flipped it on. She punched a few buttons until a loud rock song filled the car. Then she closed her eyes and crossed her arms, silently dismissing him.

Troy reluctantly shook his head and focused on the road. He'd been called a lot of things in his life, by a lot of different women...some of whom had been hurling objects at him as well as words.

But he'd never known a woman whose insults made him want her even more.

4

VENUS GOT HER FIRST real indication about just how much Max Longotti might be worth when she saw his house. House, though, probably wasn't the right word. Friggin' mansion would be more appropriate.

Her jaw fell open as they drove up the long, tree-lined driveway of the estate, which was just north of the city in a pretty, trendy area called Buckhead. "Holy crap, the old guy with the mail-order business lives *here?* Or is this a hotel?"

"No, Max lives here. Alone. Longotti Lines is a little more than a mail-order business," Troy replied, sounding amused. "It's one of the top catalog retailers in the U.S. Right up there with Land's End and the other biggies."

She whistled, tilting her head back to look to the top of the graceful, two-story house with the thick, round columns across the front. Maybe her Scarlett act hadn't been so far off. The place did remind her of an old-fashioned plantation house, surrounded by rolling green lawn and lush landscaping.

A small balcony with an intricate lattice railing ran across the entire front of the building, above the porch, and curved around the sides as well. Huge French doors provided access from what were probably upstairs bedrooms.

A queasy knot formed in her stomach. She could already picture a forty-foot-long dining-room table, each place set with a dozen metal torture devices masquerading as silverware. There'd probably be an obsequious waiter standing behind every diner, ready to swoop down on anyone who dared to lick a little drop of gravy off her finger or, heaven forbid, sneeze into a pressed linen napkin.

"I feel sick," she whispered.

Though she was speaking more to herself, she realized Troy had heard when his hand touched hers. The contact was fleeting, over so quickly, she almost suspected she'd imagined it. But when she saw his warmly concerned expression, she knew she hadn't. "You'll be fine, Venus. It's just a house."

She shook her head. "I know that," she said, trying to sound confident. "I just don't particularly care for the highbrow set."

He looked like he didn't believe her, as if he'd seen the moment of panic she'd tried to hide.

She laughed lightly. "Believe me, this is no sweat. But I am much happier slinging beer at Flanagan's, and I should be pounding the pavement to find a new job."

"Who are you trying to convince? Me or yourself?"

She shot him a glare and crossed her arms. "I should have known better than to accept a free trip from a guy I knew was too smarmy to be legit from the minute I laid eyes on him last week. Because this free vacation obviously came with a whole bunch of pricey strings attached."

He stared at her intently. "You just met Leo last week?"

She nodded, glancing back at the house. "Last Wednesday. And I knew from the minute I saw him he was up to something."

"Yet here you are."

She shrugged. She wasn't about to explain to this man, who already thought so badly of her, that she'd accepted Leo's five thousand dollars for this trip. Whether she'd taken the money to help Maureen and the kids and to keep a roof over her own head or not, he'd still think her an opportunistic money-grubber, especially if she admitted she really did not believe she was this old guy's long-lost grandchild.

Who cares what Mr. Stuffed Shirt thinks?

As much as she hated to admit it, even to herself, Venus did care. That was a strange feeling for her, considering she seldom gave a rat's ass what other people thought of her. She'd long ago decided she was comfortable in her own skin, happy with the person she'd turned out to be. Maybe a little loud. Maybe a little too friendly with too many guys. But still, a smart, hardworking, loyal woman who, until right now, had never been intimidated by anything as silly as a big ol' house in an unfamiliar city—which probably had diamond-studded chandeliers and gold-plated toilets.

"I need a drink," she muttered.

"Good, you can make us both one," Troy answered as he opened his door to step out. "Let's see how good you are at your job."

"It's just a night job," she clarified as she got out, not waiting for him to open the car door, though he'd come around to do so. "A temporary one until I can find something more permanent again." Then she thought about what he'd said. "You're staying for a while, then?" She nibbled her lip, glancing back and forth between Troy, who was at least somewhat familiar, and this house, populated probably by a bunch of absolute strangers.

He answered with a secretive smile, "Oh, yes, I'm staying."

"Suit yourself," she murmured, trying not to let him know she was pleased at not being dumped at the door.

Max Longotti had obviously phoned home and informed his housekeeper, Mrs. Harris, of Venus's arrival. The woman was welcoming and professional, greeting Troy with familiarity and Venus with unexpected warmth. Venus managed to keep her mouth closed and her eyes in her head as they walked through the huge tiled foyer. Fancy sculptures stood on tiny tables. Even fancier pictures hung on the walls. The predominant color seemed to be bluish-purple, even right down to some immense flower-filled vases that stood as high as her chin.

"Wonder if that's where they stash the bodies," she muttered.

Mrs. Harris gave her a curious look over her shoulder, and Venus bit her lip.

When Troy informed Mrs. Harris they wanted to step into Max's office for a drink, the woman took them there, telling Venus she'd be back shortly to show her to her rooms.

"Rooms?" Venus said when she and Troy were once again alone in an office that was bigger than the apartment she'd grown up in. She walked around it, trailing her fingertips across the spines of dozens of leatherbound books lining built-in mahogany shelves. The room was furnished with exquisitely detailed antique furniture; she was almost afraid to sit down.

"There are some nice guest suites upstairs. I'm sure Max has left instructions for you to be given one of them."

"Do you think he told the servants..." She lowered her head and glanced away.

He leaned a hip against a brown leather sofa, watching her, looking as comfortable in these surroundings as anyone born with a silver spoon in his mouth. Unlike Venus, in her too-skimpy, too-tight shorts and her suggestive shirt, who probably looked like she should have come in through the service entrance.

"Told them what?" Troy asked. "Who you are? Or, who you *might* be?"

She nodded, hoping he'd say no, that she wouldn't have to act out this charade in front of a bunch of servants who might very well have known Mr. Longotti's long-lost son. The last thing she needed was to be watched by every person in the place, her every move evaluated, her every word analyzed.

"I doubt it's common knowledge," Troy said, making her hopes rise. "But I would imagine Mrs. Harris knows. She's worked for Max for decades."

She sighed and glanced at the closed door through which the housekeeper had exited. "She was awfully nice. Do you think she knows...knew...Max's son?"

He nodded. "I would imagine."

"Great," she muttered. "No wonder she was friendly."

"So," he said, raising a questioning brow, "you're trying to tell me you're really *not* anxious to be greeted as the prodigal granddaughter?"

She snorted and shot him a look telling him just how stupid he was even to have asked. He didn't seem offended. Instead, he walked toward her, crossing the room in a few long strides. His hard body did lovely things for the well-tailored suit.

Though she'd more often dated men who wore jeans and leather, there was something intoxicating about seeing a thoroughly male animal—with an occasional hint of wildness in his eyes—wrapped up in an elegant, sophisticated package like Troy's conservative gray suit. It almost challenged a woman, as if luring her into stepping closer to a beautiful but caged tiger. Until the woman found out the cage door was open and the magnificent animal ready to spring.

She'd tried to tell herself Troy Langtree was a stuffed shirt. But she couldn't erase what had happened on the balcony when they first met. He'd been smooth, charming, intense. Sexy as pure sin. His kiss had completely seduced her. While safe in his arms, she'd wanted to make love with him more than she'd wanted to draw another breath.

Just because he'd repressed that part of himself ever since finding out who she was didn't mean it no longer existed. She saw it in his eyes, in the self-assured way he carried that long, lean body. For some wicked reason, it only made her more determined to find it again. Someday, when she had her confidence back.

"Are you curious about him?" Troy asked. "Max's son?"

Crossing her arms tightly over her chest, Venus forced herself to take a deep breath. She sat on the arm of a high, wing-backed chair and feigned nonchalance. "I suppose. Wouldn't anyone be?"

Instead of answering, he gestured toward a massive wooden desk near one of the huge arched windows overlooking the side lawn. The late-afternoon sunlight dripped in, illuminating the fine grain of the wood on the desktop, which was almost the same color as his thick hair. She noticed the back of a decorative, silver picture frame just as Troy said, "There's a photo of him on the desk."

She tightened her arms, almost hugging herself. "I don't think so. Maybe later."

Venus was the one who was supposed to make the drinks, but instead Troy moved to a discreet corner bar and poured two shots of whiskey. After returning with them, he handed her one. "You can impress me with your bartending skills another time. You look like you could use this."

Though she hated confirming how wildly unstable her emotions were, she took the crystal glass gratefully. She tossed it back, feeling the warmth of the amber liquid ooze through her body almost instantly. Closing her eyes, she took a deep breath.

"Good Scotch."

"Another?"

She shook her head.

When he took the empty glass from her hand, his fingers brushed against hers, sending more heat rushing through her body than the alcohol had. He seemed just as aware, standing close, holding the empty tumbler in his fingers and staring at her intently. Finally, he leaned over to place their glasses on a small, decorative table. His body was so close to hers, for a brief moment she could feel his breath on her cheek and his pant legs brushing her thigh.

He straightened, but didn't move away. "I would think if you were really curious you'd want to see what he looked like," he said softly. "So do you really not care?" He narrowed his eyes. "Or is it that you're afraid?"

"I'm not afraid," she insisted.

But even as she said the words, she knew she was lying.

She *was* afraid—though probably not for the reason

Troy thought. She couldn't explain it to him, though. Hell, she could barely admit it to herself.

He might think she feared looking at the picture and seeing a stranger with not one feature like hers. Feared not having any support for Leo's claims. In actuality, Venus dreaded the thought of her own eyes staring back at her. She didn't *want* to recognize the curve of the man's smile, or think his chin resembled hers. She couldn't bear it if the widow's peak on her forehead had been inherited from him.

This whole idea—a fat paycheck for an all-expenses paid vacation—had never seemed more dangerous than right now.

No, she was nowhere near ready to look at that man's picture. Not when seeing it might provide more evidence of the death of a parent she'd never met. She'd remain happily in the dark for as long as she could. Hopefully long enough to fully earn the five grand and hightail it back to Baltimore, with a nice, friendly wave to an elderly gentleman who was *not* her grandfather!

Stepping within inches of her body, Troy made a quiet assessment of her face, looking searchingly into her eyes, which, she suspected, were overly bright right now. Finally, he tilted his head and said in an almost wondering tone, "You're afraid you'll see something you recognize, aren't you? You really *don't* want it to be true."

He didn't say another word, letting his words hang there between them. He didn't expect her to answer, obviously knowing what she'd say.

"Why, Venus?" He shook his head, still appearing surprised by his own insight. "I don't get this."

She had no doubt of that. Troy wanted to figure out why a woman from the wrong side of the tracks wasn't rubbing her hands together in glee at her current situation. Most women would probably be thrilled to discover they could be an heiress. Most would at least be happy finally to know the truth about their parentage.

But Venus wasn't like most. Never had been. Never would be.

"I don't fit in here. I belong in this world about as much as a priest belongs in a synagogue," she said with a dry chuckle, giving him only part of the explanation. She wondered why she bothered trying to make him understand even that much, why she cared what he thought. "I don't know the language. I don't know the customs. I don't have the right clothes, the right speech, the right hair or the right attitude." She shook her head. Voicing these minor misgivings almost made her forget the major ones. "At this moment, Troy, I'm seriously wishing to God I'd never come. This was a stupid idea and I was nuts to go along with it."

He didn't say anything for a moment, just continued to look at her. It was unnerving, having all that intense, masculine attention focused squarely on her face. His shimmering green eyes darkened as he stared at her. Her heart sped up in her chest, reacting to his closeness, to the warmth of his body and his spicy scent.

Remembering the way he'd tasted on her tongue.

Venus had never once, not in her entire life, wanted to melt into a man's arms only to be held and taken care of. She'd been in men's arms for passion. For possession. For desire. For need. And yes, she knew she wanted all those things from this man she'd only known a matter of hours.

But, right now, his tender concern seemed pretty damned attractive, too. Particularly when he reached up to brush a long strand of hair off her brow, his touch innocent yet crackling with electricity.

He leaned closer. "I understand." Then, to her further

surprise, he continued. "You're not alone, Venus. I'm going to help you."

AN HOUR LATER, while taking a long shower that did nothing to cool his overheated skin, Troy still couldn't believe he'd offered to help Venus.

"Help her do what?" he muttered as he reached out to turn the spray from lukewarm to cool. He know what he *really* wanted to help her do.

Have a whole bunch of screaming orgasms.

But that was out. No screaming orgasms loomed in the future for either one of them. Not even here in a large, dual-headed shower where he probably should have blown off some sexual steam before he saw the beautiful redhead again.

Troy didn't want to blow off steam with his hand. He wanted to create some serious steam...with her.

Why he wanted her so much, he really couldn't say. She was amazing to look at, sure, but he interacted with attractive women all the time. And for the past three months, none of them had come close to luring him out of his unintentional celibacy. Venus had done it with a flick of her ankle as she tapped her shoe into the air on the balcony.

His suspicions about her should have tamped down on the desire. They hadn't. The fact that she was a mystery—a cocky, confident mystery—had only added to the instant heat he'd felt when he first laid eyes on her.

Well, not entirely confident. Obviously the woman's self-confidence had taken a real hit when she'd arrived here at Max's home. In the library, when he'd attempted to look at it from her point of view, he'd felt for her. Not that Max would care—if she really were his granddaughter, he wouldn't give a damn whether she fit into his world or not.

Venus, however, quite obviously cared. It couldn't have been easy for a proud woman to admit she couldn't handle the situation in which she found herself. The confusion and hint of fear in her eyes had affected him more deeply than he'd ever have imagined possible. He saw a hint of vulnerability in her which she'd probably never admit to having.

And, to be honest, he admired her. She didn't seem at all bitter, despite the bits and pieces he'd managed to glean about her life. She'd been orphaned, raised in foster care and had had to fight for every single thing she got. Yet it hadn't made her greedy or grasping, nor had it made her resentful. She had a genuine smile and an infectious laugh. Her smart mouth was buoyed by an innate sense of humor that said she didn't take anything too seriously.

Completely unlike him.

Troy was well used to being around money. He, more than anyone, knew he'd been incredibly fortunate to have always been part of a wealthy lifestyle. Still, he liked to think it hadn't ruined him. He might have a reputation as a playboy at night, but fifty-hour workweeks had been a part of his life for the past several years. He didn't mind hard work though, since he had never aspired to be a useless rich guy with fast cars, fast women and no ambition.

He also liked to think he could do exactly what his twin had—make it completely on his own, without a penny of Langtree money. Though until recently his paychecks had come from a family-owned business, that's essentially what he'd done. His salary had certainly been in line with any other retail executive, and it had supported him just fine. He wore nice clothes because he liked them and got them at a discount. He drove a Jaguar because he enjoyed going fast. Otherwise, he was pretty conservative with his money.

Not, he imagined, that Venus Messina would believe it.

Whatever she believed, she had to know he was in a position to help her deal with her new surroundings. If Leo's claims proved true, if she really was Max's granddaughter, she'd have to deal with them for the rest of her life.

Tending bar at a Baltimore pub was a long way from interacting with the elite of Atlanta. She was right—she'd be crucified the minute she attended her first social function. Not by Max, of course. If Venus really turned out to be his son's daughter, Max wouldn't care if the woman got up and danced the limbo on the bar at the country club.

"She won't, though," he muttered as he rinsed his hair. Because Troy had said he'd help her and that's exactly what he intended to do. At least until he found out for sure what she was up to. Until then, helping her learn to fit in would be the perfect excuse to keep her within his sight and try to make sure Max didn't get hurt. The tricky part would be keeping her in his sight...but out of his arms and out of his bed.

Which was exactly where he most wanted her to be.

She was funny and beautiful. Irreverent and bawdy. But at some moments so damned vulnerable, he wanted to just take her in his arms and hold her. Pretty unbelievable for Troy Langtree, whose own twin had on occasion called him a louse when it came to women.

Twisting the knob close to ice-cold, he let a jet of frigid water cascade down his body, then turned the shower off. After opening the glass door, he stepped out onto the mat, then reached for a towel he'd dropped on the counter earlier. Before he could take another step toward it, however, he realized he had company.

Venus.

Standing just a few feet away, inside the bathroom, she froze, just as he did. Their eyes met, their stares held. They both sucked in their breath and held it. Each stunned. Each unsure what would come next.

Troy noted the shock on her face. He didn't imagine Venus Messina was shocked by much. Now, though, her wide eyes and gaping mouth said his presence had taken her by surprise.

"Ever hear of knocking?" he asked in a lazy drawl, making no effort to grab the towel. Hell, if she wanted to stand there staring at his naked body, instead of beating a hasty retreat, he'd accommodate her.

She wore only a fluffy towel sarong style, that barely covered all the essentials. Her hair was piled loosely on her head, with a few long, tempting curls hanging loose. In one hand she held a small bottle of bath oil and a paperback book. Her other hand was pressed flat against her heart, the bright red tips of her long nails stark against the white terrycloth and her smooth, creamy skin.

Her eyes remained wide and appraising. Without so much as an apology, an embarrassed explanation, and certainly not a quick exit, she moved her gaze over his body, head to toe. Even from here he could see the strong, fast pulse in her neck and the rush of color on her face. Her every deeply inhaled breath loosened the towel she wore. His heart skipped a beat, as he wondered if the loose knot would give way, revealing her body to his hungry gaze, as his was to her.

On someone shorter, the towel might have done an adequate job of covering the critical parts of a woman's body. On Venus, it barely concealed the tips of her lush breasts, showing deep cleavage and creamy smooth skin. The tight shirt she'd worn earlier hadn't done justice to the curviness of the woman.

Troy used to consider himself a leg man. Right now, though, he'd have to say full mouthwatering breasts had jumped to the top of his list.

The bottom hem of her towel came within a whisper of reaching her upper thighs. But the fabric didn't quite conceal a shadowy hint of the curls between her legs. He swallowed a groan as his mouth went dry with pure undiluted want. His body, already in a state of semiarousal since the moment they met, reacted predictably.

She noticed, and finally regained her voice. "Oh. My. God."

Yeah. That summed it up about as well as anything else.

For a moment, Venus couldn't make sense of what had happened. She'd come strolling into the bathroom, deciding to take advantage of its sunken tub, which the housekeeper had mentioned when showing her to her own suite. And she'd walked in on the most perfectly luscious naked male body she'd ever seen.

Perfect. Luscious. Naked. Oh, yes. Oh, yes, indeedy.

Troy Langtree was a woman's centerfold fantasy in the flesh. He made her remember why she was so very glad to be a woman without even touching her.

He had the kind of thickly muscled shoulders that made her fingers tighten at the thought of digging into them. His chest was just as strong, perfectly sinewed and rippling, with flat, male nipples puckered from his shower. Her own nipples tightened beneath the towel, sending a sharp sense of awareness ratcheting throughout her.

Water dripped from his hair to his shoulders, then lower, riding the muscles down his body. They were like precise, tiny arrows she wanted to follow with her tongue.

Follow the arrows to the treasure.

The very bountiful treasure.

Her mouth went dry. And moisture gathered between her legs. Her desire raged insistent and hot, begging for the kind of release only a man—*this* man—could give her.

Somehow, though, Venus remained upright and continued examining him.

His skin was tanned. She figured that made sense because he'd lived at the beach in Florida. But the physique was a definite surprise. Troy Langtree was toned and muscular, hot and hard. Not at all the suit-wearing businessman type she'd have expected. This guy had the kind of body that could make a grown woman sit up and beg.

Wiry dark hair swirled over his chest, around the nipples she wanted to taste with her tongue and down the washboard stomach. Then lower, trailing in a thin line, stark against the paler skin below the edge of his tan. It took a lot of self-control to keep from sighing as she looked even farther, holding her breath as his very impressive male package swelled under her hot, appreciative stare.

Watching him grow fully erect, until he was throbbing and ready, she dropped her book and bath oil, and clutched the counter for support.

Women weren't supposed to react this way, were they? Good women were supposed to want protestations of love. Roses. Candlelight. Whispered promises meant to be broken. Tender touches and kisses. A connection of the heart before a connection of the body.

Hell, at least dinner and a movie first!

But Venus just wanted *that*. That magnificent hard-on Troy Langtree made absolutely no effort to disguise, not to mention all the rest of his big, hard body.

"Are you lost?" he finally asked, still completely in control, making no effort to cover himself, showing no sign of embarrassment at his obvious reaction to her.

She shook her head mindlessly. "Mrs....um...the housekeeper..."

"Mrs. Harris?"

She nodded. "When she took me to my room, she told me to feel free to use any parts of the house I wanted."

"Including my bathroom?"

She gulped. "I didn't know it was yours. She said my room has the best view, but apologized because the bathroom has a standard tub. And she said this room had a great sunken tub with massaging jets."

"It does," he said, glancing toward the tub a few feet away. "You'd love it." His words sounded almost like an invitation to try it out.

"I had no idea anyone would be in here since you said Max lives alone. I thought I'd take a bath...I didn't realize..."

"I'm a houseguest this week too."

"I'm sorry to intrude."

"Sorry enough to hand me a towel?"

"Only an idiot would be *that* sorry," she mumbled, unable to remove her eyes from his naked form.

Casting a quick glimpse at his face, she saw his eyes darken. A small smile widened his lips.

"So you strolled right down the hall," he continued

with a pointed look at her towel, which, even she could admit, didn't cover much. "Like that?"

"I'm right next door. Your door's four feet from mine," she replied, hearing the breathy tone in her voice. "It was a spur-of-the-moment kind of decision."

The explanation sounded weak, even to her own ears. But it was entirely true. With every step she'd taken as Max Longotti's housekeeper had led her toward her room, she'd grown more and more convinced she could never be comfortable in this house. There was too much money and too much class, from the roof on down to the pricey tile, for Venus Messina to ever feel comfortable.

A bath had sounded downright necessary.

A naked man *and* a bath sounded downright delightful. She very much wanted both. One after the other or both at the same time. Any way she could have them.

He finally chuckled. "Do you really think this is fair?"

"Fair?"

"I mean, is it fair for you to see what you do to me? Just the thought of you made my shower a lot more chilly than it would otherwise have been."

He had to take a cold shower for her? Damn, that was a pretty high compliment, in Venus's opinion.

"Men are pretty obvious about things like this," she finally admitted as she stole another peek at the impressive evidence he made no effort to hide.

"So are women."

She raised a brow. "Oh?"

He grinned lazily. "It's a little more concealed, but it's just as easy for a man to see a woman's desire...if he knows what he's looking for."

She instantly reacted to the note of challenge in his voice. "Oh, really? And I suppose you're an expert?"

He shrugged. "Maybe."

She had no doubt this man knew his way with women. But Venus also knew women's bodies were neater, much more discreet than men's. Just glancing at his made that perfectly clear.

Crossing her arms, she retorted, "Aside from the one obvious point, which could also be caused by a chill, I'm not buying it."

He looked pleased, as if her words had led her directly into his trap. When he continued, she realized they had.

"There's one way to prove it," he murmured, his eyes holding a recognizable spark of mischief.

"Drop the towel."

5

VENUS NIBBLED HER LIP, noting the amused challenge in his voice. He almost certainly didn't think she'd do it. After all, she'd walked in on him by accident, and he hadn't intentionally exposed himself to her.

This was different. What woman would simply drop her towel in broad daylight and show her naked body to a man she'd known for only a few hours? A man with whom she had no relationship and had never been intimate?

Nudity with a new lover was intimidating enough. This bordered on exhibitionism.

It would take a lot of confidence, and a lot more nerve.

Fortunately, Venus had been blessed with both.

She reached for the knot over her breast, never taking her eyes from his. He raised a brow, silently egging her on.

"You think I won't?"

"I think you want me to *think* you will," he countered.

She wondered if the naked hunk had retained any of his normal executive, suit-wearing inhibitions now that his clothes were off. If so, she'd be able to tell by his reaction. Right now.

Untying the towel, she removed her hand and let gravity do the rest.

A slow, pleased smile spread across his parted lips as he studied her from head to toe. Not a hint of shock appeared on his face; he never even pretended to look away.

Question answered. No inhibitions in the man.

Venus remained still, letting him look his fill, knowing what he saw. Full breasts, slim waist, flat tummy as a result of way more sit-ups than any one person should have to endure. Her hips were a little rounder than she'd like, but not bad for a woman pushing thirty. And she already knew he liked her legs—he'd been eyeing them since the minute they met.

She heard him draw in a ragged breath. He obviously approved.

"You didn't think I'd do it, did you?"

He tilted his head and raised a brow. "Oh, I *knew* you'd do it, Venus. Why else do you think I suggested it?"

He wasn't kidding. He'd known damn well she wouldn't back down from his challenge. He hadn't known her long, but he already knew her better than most other people ever had.

"Okay, you got me naked. Now, big shot," she said, narrowing her eyes in challenge, "are you going to wow me with your expertise on women?"

He stepped closer, moving noiselessly across the bathmat, until they were less than a foot apart. She could feel his warm breath on her cheek and see the pulse in his temple. That gorgeous erection was within inches of where she wanted it. Her body arched forward the tiniest bit, of its own will.

Schooling herself to remain calm, she figured her tightly clenched fingers on the counter were about the only indication of the inferno raging inside her body.

"Your eyes are glassy, your pupils dilated and your lids half lowered."

She blinked twice. "Bad lighting."

He laughed softly at the lie.

"Your lips are pursed," Troy said, his voice low and soothing, almost melodic. "You're thinking of being kissed. Of kissing back. Of using your mouth for something other than talking. Lots of somethings."

Score one for the men's team.

"Pursed lips can also be a sign of attitude," she countered weakly.

He nodded. "Oh, honey, there's no question you've got miles of attitude." Watching as he moistened his own lips with his tongue, she nearly moaned. "But it's not your attitude at work when your lips are full and ripe and parted like that. It's another part of Venus altogether."

Yeah. The empty, aching part that badly needed to be filled by him.

He stared into her eyes for a long moment, and she knew he saw the truth she couldn't possibly hide. Then he looked lower. His breaths grew more labored—she heard each one as he drew it into his mouth and slowly exhaled, as if striving for control when there was none to be found.

He stared at her bare throat. Her shoulders. The nape of her neck, where one long curl brushed her collarbone.

Then he studied her breasts, which felt heavier and tighter under his hungry gaze. "It's not too cold in here," he murmured, "so you couldn't have a chill."

True, she acknowledged silently. Her nipples tightened even more, drawing into pointy tips as she imagined him using his mouth on them.

"That's almost too easy, though," he continued. "So let's move on. There's a pink glow on your skin. You're flushed and breathing in shallow breaths, because you're so excited."

She closed her eyes, trying to relax, but unable to.

"Your stomach is quivering slightly with the effort it's taking you to keep your body stiff and unyielding when it wants to be loose and pliant."

She moaned softly, but didn't open her eyes. She kept focusing on his voice, trying not to think of how much she wanted to reach out a few inches and let her fingers do some walking.

"Though you're trying to stand straight, your legs are shaky. I can see the muscles straining beneath your skin."

When she felt a butterfly-light touch on her thigh, her eyes flew open. "I didn't think touching was part of the demonstration," she said between ragged breaths.

"It's not. I don't have to touch you to know how much you want me." He moved his hand again, the tips of his fingers scraping ever so delicately across the curls concealing her womanhood. "Though, if I did, I think we'd both see just how much you do."

She nodded, knowing exactly where he could touch her to prove his point. She was so wet and throbbing, she'd come apart at his slightest touch. The mere thought of him sliding his fingers into her made her moan slightly.

"Do you concede?" he whispered, still holding his hand no more than a centimeter from her curls. "I am correct in thinking you're incredibly aroused right now?"

She nodded, unable to lie to him any more than she could to herself. "I concede."

Oh, yes, she was definitely aroused right now, so aroused she would have gone for it, right here and now, hard and fast up against the sink. Then slow and languorous in the bathtub. Even having only known him for only a matter of hours, she would have. If it weren't for three things: location, location, location.

"So I want you. And you want me too," she whispered.

He didn't try to deny it. "I've wanted you since the moment I saw your pretty ankles when you were sitting on the balcony outside my office." The smooth words couldn't hide the intensity in the man's voice.

Venus had been desired before. She'd had sex before. She'd even had relationships before. But she'd never felt like someone wanted to inhale her completely, to indulge in her body and give her every bit of primal passion a man was capable of.

Until right now.

"Point taken. We want each other," she said raggedly. "But this would really complicate things with the old man, wouldn't it? For both of us." Part of her wanted him not to care. A bigger part knew he couldn't.

At his frustrated groan, she continued. "This was a pretty damn stupid thing to start when we know we're not going to finish it." *Are we?* She heard the tone in her voice that almost made her comment sound like a question.

He looked at her for one moment longer, then his eyes shifted away. She heard him mutter a curse under his breath and nearly echoed it.

"You're right. Incredibly stupid." He thrust a frustrated hand through his still-wet hair, sending droplets of water onto her hot skin, providing instant, shocking sensation. He picked up a towel from the counter and slung it around his lean hips.

"I'm sorry, Venus."

Hearing him acknowledge that, no, they were not going to finish the way they both wanted to, she sighed heavily. Not wanting to tempt fate by retrieving the towel she'd dropped by bending down in front of this gloriously erect man, she grabbed a fresh one from a rack behind her. Quickly, she wrapped it around her.

When covered, she forced a laugh. "Considering I haven't had an orgasm that didn't involve a vibrator in so long I've forgotten what one feels like, you're probably not as sorry as I am."

His mouth opened and he gaped at her, as if completely unable to believe she'd said what she'd said. *Okay, that was probably a little crass for Mr. V.P.*

Then she realized he hadn't been shocked by her language.

"You can't tell me you haven't had a lover for a long time. You are the most sensuous, desirable woman I've ever met, Venus. I have trouble believing you couldn't have any man you wanted, any time you wanted him."

I can't have you.

"It's been a long time. Since last fall," she admitted, lowering her lashes and wondering why she'd confessed something so intimate. Maybe because her heart had skipped a beat or two when he'd called her the most desirable woman he'd ever met.

Flattery had been known to make women do foolish things before.

He didn't answer right away. Instead, he stepped closer, then closer still. His expression was intense, focused. His eyes flared with heat and determination. Wary, she took a tiny step back, but was blocked by the vanity countertop behind her.

"That's too damn long," he said, his voice thick and husky.

Before she knew his intention, he'd slipped his hand

into her hair, tangling it in his fingers. He drew her close, catching her surprised cry with his lips.

His kiss was hotter than the one they'd shared earlier, on the balcony. Hot and hungry, and Venus melted against him. He made love to her mouth with his tongue until she began to whimper, needing more, wanting more than they'd just agreed they could have.

He slid his palm down her bare arm, slowly, his fingertips creating heat and electricity on her skin, then lower, until his hand brushed against her towel-covered hip.

She jerked and gasped. He only kissed her deeper. When his hand moved between the edges of the towel to brush against her naked thigh, she knew what he was doing, what he wanted to give her. She had one second to wrap her mind around it before his hot fingers slipped between her legs. "Oh, God," she managed to cry, feeling the pressure. She arched into his hand, growing even more mindless when she heard his groan of pure male satisfaction at feeling how wet she was. For him.

"Oh, Troy...*please*," she whispered brokenly.

He teased her, sending her higher as he made tantalizing circles around her throbbing clitoris. When she thought she'd burst with frustration, he gave her a little more, slipping his finger inside her, mimicking the movement with his tongue.

She began to shake, until finally he whispered against her lips, "Now, honey. Right now."

Finally he zeroed in on her hottest spot. With just a few perfect strokes on the delicate flesh, he gave her exactly what she'd been missing. She cried out as waves of pleasure ratcheted through her body, the orgasm literally making her shake so hard he had to support her in his arms.

He kept kissing her, taking her cries against his lips as

she gradually returned to sanity. It took several long moments. The intensity of her climax had been like nothing she'd ever experienced before.

"It's funny," he whispered as he moved his mouth to kiss her cheek, then her eyelid. "Right before you came in, I'd been thinking about how much I wanted to give you a bunch of screaming orgasms."

"One down," she managed to mutter, not sure where she got the strength to use her voice.

He chuckled. Pressing one more kiss against her temple, he stepped back. She instantly missed the hot, hard feel of his body against hers. "Troy?"

"You should go," he murmured, gently pushing her toward the open door. She couldn't even protest as he gently shuffled her out into her bedroom. Then, he stepped back inside the bathroom. "I somehow think I need to take another shower. A long one." His eyelids lowered slightly, as did his voice. "I can pretty much guarantee what I'll be thinking about for every minute of it." He shut the door before she could protest.

Venus stood there, listening to the lock click, then the shower turn on. She knew what he was doing.

And she wished like hell she was the one doing it for him.

AFTER TAKING another long and equally unsatisfying shower, Troy dressed for dinner. Though an easygoing man, Max did enjoy the niceties and, so far, every night Troy had been here they'd had a full-course dinner in the dining room. Tonight, he found himself hoping the salad forks weren't too confusing. The quiet, elegant dinner hour might never be the same once Venus got through with it.

Venus. He closed his eyes, pausing while shrugging on

his pressed white shirt. He still couldn't get her image out of his mind. Like her namesake, she was the epitome of woman, so damned seductive he had been barely able to shut the door behind her after pushing her away earlier.

He'd known full well she wouldn't be able to resist his challenge when he practically dared her to drop the towel. Probably not his wisest move. It had been bad enough when he'd only imagined what she looked like under her clothes. Now, having seen her, all he could think about was what it would be like to go farther. Her body was the kind men fantasized about—lushly curved, sleek and supple. He wanted nothing on earth as much as he wanted to cup her breasts, to suck those tight nipples into his mouth, to press hot kisses on her stomach...and hotter ones between her long, pale thighs.

Not taking her while she still shook from her orgasm had required every bit of self-control he possessed.

"Cool it, jackass," he muttered aloud, knowing there was no time for yet another shower this evening. Hell, when his sex drive came back, it came back with a vengeance.

He was dying to make love to her. Kissing her, touching her, catching her cries of pleasure in his mouth may have given *her* a little release from the tension, but it had only added to his. Troy knew he'd be able to think of nothing else but making love with Venus every time he was with her.

And when he wasn't with her he'd have the memory of how she'd looked when she'd dropped the towel. Not just her glorious body, but that spark of devilment and outright confidence in her eyes that he'd never before encountered with another woman.

No question, if she'd been anybody else, he would

have made love to her right there on the bathroom counter an hour ago. They'd probably be in the middle of their second or third encounter right now.

"Not happening," he reminded himself. *Unfortunately.*

A few minutes later, after he was dressed and back in control of his raging hormones, Troy left his room. Noticing Venus's open door and empty suite, he headed downstairs alone. The house was quiet, and he wondered if Max and Leo had returned. Spying Mrs. Harris in the foyer, he asked her.

"Mr. Longotti is in with *her*," the gray-haired woman said in a loud whisper, nodding toward the closed office door.

"Is he all right?"

She frowned, nearly clucking in disapproval. "He looked very pale and tired when he and Mr. Gallagher returned." The way the housekeeper said Leo's name hinted at what she thought of the man. "Too much excitement."

"I would suspect Ms. Messina's arrival was quite a surprise for him," Troy said, not wanting to put the woman in an uncomfortable position, but needing to see if she could provide any useful information. After all, she knew Max better than just about anybody else. "I'm sure it will make him very happy, though, if it turns out to be true, and she is his grandchild."

"Of course it will," the woman replied. "Never was a man who loved his son more than Mr. Longotti. Losing him the way he did, so soon after he'd lost Miss Violet...it wasn't fair."

Troy tilted his head in confusion. "Miss Violet?"

The woman nodded. "Mrs. Longotti."

That explained why the name Violet had been important on the back of the mysterious baby photo. And why Max had been so keenly interested in Venus's name.

"She passed on when Max Jr. was in high school," Mrs. Harris continued, "just a few years before he left. I often thought that's why he went. Mr. Longotti couldn't let her go. He repainted the house, filled it with different shades of violet, and Max Jr. couldn't stand the constant reminders."

Troy knew Max was a widower, but didn't realize how long ago he'd lost his wife. No wonder the man seemed so alone. He *had* been for a very long time. "Sad," he murmured.

Mrs. Harris nodded and lowered her voice further. "Yes, it is. Which is why I'm hoping Mr. Gallagher knows what he's doing. I don't think Mr. Longotti could handle another loss. He's not been well, anyway. If he grows to care about this young woman, and she turns out not to be Max's daughter, he's going to be badly hurt. He could break down again...."

She quickly glanced away, as if realizing she'd said too much. Troy certainly wasn't going to pry.

At that moment, movement in the front living room caught his eye. Leo stood there, staring absently out the window.

Perfect. Troy very much wanted to speak with the man. After thanking Mrs. Harris, he joined Leo, pausing to make himself a drink at the well-stocked wet bar.

"How was Max's appointment?" he asked, keeping a note of casual interest in his voice as he took a seat on one of the overstuffed sofas.

"All right," Leo replied, his lips twisted into what probably was supposed to be a smile. "He has to have some more tests later in the week. He's too old to work himself as hard as he does and the doctors are concerned."

The man still stood at the window, moving his gaze between the lawn and Troy.

"Quite a shock he got today."

Leo nodded. "Oh, yes. I haven't seen Uncle Max quite so pleased in a long, long time."

"Yes, I'm sure. How fortunate you were to find the missing child after all these years." Troy paused to sip his drink. "When did you say you came up with the idea to have an investigator look in the New York area?"

Leo visibly stiffened. "Recently. I didn't want to raise Uncle Max's hopes, though, which is why I didn't mention it until I had all the information."

"And everything happened to occur last week." *Just two days after I arrived.*

"Yes." The man smiled thinly. "How unfortunate that you came up here to Atlanta for nothing."

"Oh? I don't understand," Troy said, though he understood full well where Leo was headed.

"Well," the man explained, "it's possible Max will rethink his strategy. He does, after all, have a grandchild to think of."

"You mean you don't think he'll sell?"

Before Leo could answer, a door opened and warm laughter filled the foyer. Troy watched intently, seeing Max exit his office with Venus on his arm.

Venus. Troy had to lower his head to hide a chuckle when he saw her. She looked positively wicked in a short black leather skirt that showed off long bare legs to perfection. A flouncy white peasant blouse hung right at the edges of her shoulders. Her high-heeled black shoes made her tower over Max. And her hair was poufed up in a mass of curls which added another couple of inches to her already considerable height.

Judging by the look on his face, Max didn't seem to care. He looked completely delighted in her company.

"Troy, Leo," he said as they entered the room, "you must have Venus tell you how she and her foster family used to use the Longotti Lines catalog to decorate their home."

Leo raised an arrogant brow. "I didn't imagine your childhood home to be the type in need of interior design."

Troy stiffened, wondering if the guy had to work hard at always sounding like a pretentious ass.

Max ignored his nephew and took a seat on a sofa near the front window. "Troy, as I was saying, Venus and her foster mother were big fans of our catalogs. They used to cut out the pictures and tape them to the walls. They'd redo the look of their entire apartment every season."

Venus grinned. "Can I confess that it wasn't always the Longotti Lines catalog?"

Max put his index finger over his lips and frowned. "Shh. Don't ruin the story."

"Sorry. But, frankly, we were limited to the catalogs the doctors had on the tables in the waiting room at the health clinic—because we had to steal 'em, of course."

"Very nice," Leo murmured.

She smirked, obviously enjoying goading Leo, who was so blatant in his disapproval.

"Don't you need to get home?" Max asked Leo, giving him a pointed stare. "Your mother said you were supposed to take her to the club this evening."

That was another thing Troy couldn't stand about Leo. The man still lived with his mother, for God's sake.

"Yes, I should," Leo replied. "Now, Uncle Max, don't

forget to take your pills," he said. "And please you mustn't forget again about your next appointment."

He left quickly, pausing only long enough to bid a pleasant goodbye to Max and Venus and a not-so-friendly one to Troy.

"He makes my teeth hurt," the old man muttered once Leo was gone.

Venus snorted a laugh, as if she understood exactly what Max meant. Considering the number of times he'd clenched his jaw when Leo was around, Troy thought he did, too.

"Treats me like I'm an imbecile," Max continued. "I tell myself he means well. He took over quite a lot—a little *too* much—when he said I kept forgetting appointments or missing deadlines." Max glanced at Troy and gave him an approving nod. "Now, I have you to do that, though."

"Yes, you do," Troy said, "and I'll update you after dinner on some of the meetings I had this morning."

Max shrugged, as if uninterested. "I tried to like Leo when my brother married his mother. He was five or six then." He stroked his jaw absently as he stared out the front window. "But I just couldn't take to the kind of kid who'd constantly torment my boy with wet willies and arm burns, or run and tattle whenever Maxie did the slightest thing wrong."

Maxie. Max Jr. Beside him, he saw Venus stiffen ever so slightly. No one else would even have noticed. But Troy was very much in tune to her every movement right now, particularly because of what they'd shared in his bathroom earlier.

Max gave a rather evil-sounding chuckle. "Not that my Maxie couldn't hold his own. He might have been a few years younger, but he was a quick one. Talked circles around Leo." Obviously lost in memory, he slapped his own knee in delight. "Tricked Leo into playing cowboys and tied him to a telephone pole down the road one day, just so he could get some peace from the whining, he said."

Even Venus smiled briefly. Then she glanced away, still obviously uncomfortable. Max didn't seem to notice. "I had to punish him, a'course. But my Maxie didn't have so much trouble with Leo after that day."

Before Max could comment further, Mrs. Harris stepped in to tell him he had a phone call. He picked up the receiver on a side table and quickly became engrossed in a conversation.

Informing them dinner would be ready shortly, Mrs. Harris exited, leaving Troy and Venus alone, staring at one another.

"So," Troy said, determined to steer the conversation away from Max's late son, "you covered your bedroom walls with pictures from catalogs. My twin brother always preferred those Pamela Anderson-type posters."

The tension faded from her face as she snickered. "Oh, you mean there's actually blood running through the veins of someone in your family?"

He laughed softly at the jibe, glad he'd distracted her. "You weren't complaining about me being cold-blooded an hour ago." In a soft whisper, he mimicked her. "Oh, Troy, *please.*"

"Screw you," she said with a good-natured grin.

He tsked. "I thought we already discussed that."

Apparently unwilling to be drawn into a sensual conversation, she ignored him. "I suppose you decorated your room with wide panoramic views of Fort Knox or perhaps mountains of dollar bills."

"Certainly not ones," Troy replied smoothly.

She rolled her eyes. "But, I'm sure, nothing as tasteless as pin-up girls."

"From fourteen on, I didn't *need* posters," he said, daring her to figure out what he meant.

She didn't even try. "Well, I did. When I hit my teenage years I started swiping the *People* magazines and covering my walls with pictures of Kevin Bacon and Tom Cruise."

"I assume that was before you'd reached your current height?"

"Hey, no short jokes about my honey Tom," she retorted with a chuckle. "For him, I might just rethink my 'no guys shorter or lighter than me' rule."

Troy stepped closer, until they stood nearly eye to eye. Even with her heels and poufed-up hair, she still couldn't quite match his height. He shook his head and murmured, "No, I think you're better off sticking with your rule. You need someone bigger who can keep you from walking all over him."

Her lips curved. "Better men have tried, darlin'."

"Oh, I'm sure *some* men have tried, but not *better* men." He let her see the confidence in his stare and drove his point home. "At least not for the past nine months or so."

A slow flush rose in her cheeks. Damn, he loved that he could make this unflappable woman blush. She was obviously thinking about exactly what he'd wanted her to—the way she'd felt in his arms an hour before.

She wouldn't give up, however, and whispered, "Coulda been anyone."

The dig didn't phase him. "But it wasn't, Venus." Turning slightly to block Max's view—not that the man was paying them any attention—he ran the tip of his index finger down her cheek to the corner of her full lips. "It was me."

Not giving her a chance to reply, he walked away and took a seat opposite Max. The man finished his conversation and hung up the phone. His eyes shone with interest as he stared speculatively between his houseguests. Maybe he'd been paying more attention than Troy had thought.

Troy mentally kicked himself for letting Venus get to him in front of Max. He needed to be more discreet. Unfortunately, the return of his sex drive wasn't taking into account that it wasn't very appropriate to lust after your boss's potential family members right in front of your boss.

"Can I help myself at the bar?" Venus asked Max, still looking flushed and slightly confused. Troy liked that he'd put the hungry look on her face, even as he wondered whether Max noticed.

"Please do," Max said.

Venus made her way over to the bar and poured herself a glass of wine. She glanced over her shoulder at Troy. "I owe you one, don't I?"

Glancing at his empty glass, he shrugged, wondering about the spark of mischief in the redhead's eyes. "All right, thank you," he murmured, more than ready to take her challenge.

In a few moments, she walked toward him, carrying two glasses. She pressed one into his hand, leaning close enough to whisper, "Now we're even."

They weren't anywhere close to even, not that he was going to call her on it in front of Max. Before he could think of a way to discreetly remind her of the way he'd made her come with just a few kisses and caresses, he noticed the wicked look on her face. Then he glanced lower, at the view of her perfect breasts, fully revealed when she bent over in the loose blouse.

Her bra was tiny and black. Completely wrong with a white top. Not apparently that she gave a damn. It plumped up. Pushed out. Tempted beyond belief. He almost hissed as he tried to breathe.

Her confident smile as she finally straightened and took a seat next to Max told him she knew it, too. Yes, she was definitely capable of some payback. She knew just which of his buttons to push. He apparently hadn't been very subtle in his visual appreciation of her lush breasts when she'd dropped her towel up in the bathroom.

Not that any red-blooded man could have been.

Striving for control, he finally sipped his drink. The strong flavor seemed very appropriate. Sweet, milky and creamy. Luscious but with a kick of heat—just like he imagined her soft skin would taste.

He sipped again, meeting her eye, as he licked the liquid off his lips. "It's very good," he said, making no effort to disguise the true direction of his thoughts. "I'm thirstier than I thought."

"I'm glad you like it. I'd be happy to give you another," she replied, her voice sounding a little breathless.

"So, exactly what is it?" Max asked, leaning over to stare suspiciously at the concoction.

Troy shifted in his seat, barely listening as Venus listed the ingredients. "One of my favorites. Irish Cream, coffee liqueur, almond liqueur and vodka," she explained. Then she paused, catching Troy's eye, making sure she had his undivided attention.

He had to ask, because she so wanted him to. "What's it called, Venus?"

Her wicked stare gave him a five-second warning. Then she lowered her voice to a sultry purr. "It's a screaming orgasm."

6

THOUGH THE BED was huge and comfortable, Venus slept fitfully her first night in Max Longotti's house. The comforter was one of those fancy fluffy ones that she was scared to actually use, so she folded it up and put it on a chair instead. Her window was just above a dramatic fountain on the side lawn, which gurgled and gushed all night, so she had to get up to go to the bathroom at least a half-dozen times. She sourly hoped the constant flushing kept her next-door neighbor awake.

The sheets were slick and satin instead of percale, making her wonder if she was going to slide right off the bed and knock herself unconscious. What a picture that would make for the maid in the morning. Naked Venus out cold on the floor, with a robin's egg knot on her head.

Not Venus on the half shell...Venus on a gurney.

To top it all off, the scent of lilacs wafted from a flower arrangement on the dresser. Lilacs always made her think of dead people. Not a good mental image before sleep.

No, she didn't fit in here, in spite of how much she'd enjoyed the hour she'd spent with Max Longotti in his office yesterday afternoon. The room made that obvious. As had, of course, dinner the night before.

Dinner? More like disaster.

She pulled a pillow over her face and groaned into it.

The silverware hadn't been too bad. She'd remembered what Troy said about the salad forks. And there hadn't been an army of servants, just Mrs. Harris and a maid. The table had been big, but not so huge that she couldn't talk with Max, who sat at the head, or Troy, who sat directly across from her.

But who on earth could have known the soup was supposed to be cold, the fish supposed to be raw and the pretty fruit garnish supposed to be for decoration only, not for eating? After scrunching up her nose and wondering why Max wasn't complaining about the temperature of the soup, she'd followed the lead of the men at the table and suffered through it.

There was no way, however, she could suffer through raw fish. They might call the appetizer sushi, she called it bait. She'd—very delicately, she thought—spit a mouthful of the stuff into her napkin, hiding the maneuver behind a cough.

Troy had seen, of course. When he'd rolled his eyes in disapproval, she'd considered sticking her tongue out at him, but had settled for a haughty chin lift instead.

By the time they reached the main course, she'd been so determined not to make any more faux pas that she tried to force herself to eat the undercooked roast beef, even though it was bloody enough to still be mooing.

Venus was a well-done woman.

She'd tried holding her breath while chewing really fast and had ended up nearly choking. Knocking over her wineglass while reaching for her water, she'd said a prayer the meat would cut off her oxygen supply quickly, so she'd pass out and avoid any further mortification.

No such luck. Troy, Mr. Hero, leapt around the table, hoisted her out of her chair and Heimliched her so fast she barely even saw the hunk of raw meat flying out of her mouth and into the pretty carnation centerpiece.

"At least it didn't hit Max in the head," she muttered aloud. Thank goodness for small favors. And, thankfully, Max had seemed to accept her claim that she'd had a really long day and wanted to go to her room right after dinner. Bad idea. She'd been trapped in here for hours, needing sleep the way a politician needed votes.

Though it was now only seven-thirty, she knew there was no point staying in bed. Remembering Max had said to feel free to use the pool, she decided to put on her suit and start the day with a little exercise. Though she considered exercise one of the worst words in the English language, it wasn't as bad as another of the worst words—cellulite. She'd just sat up in bed when she heard a knock on the door. "Venus?"

Troy.

Great, what a way to start the day. Face-to-face with the guy who'd seen her naked, made her have an orgasm she'd dreamed about during her pitifully few hours of sleep and sent a piece of half-chewed beef flying out of her open, drooling mouth with enough force to bruise her ribs.

"Just a sec!" She reached for the T-shirt she'd put on before going to bed last night, which, since Venus always slept naked, had been flung off within ten minutes. Unfortunately, she reached too far, and felt herself slipping right off the stupid sheets, hitting the floor with a thunk and a surprised shriek.

The door opened before she'd even had time to lift her face off the floor and see if she'd broken anything. Like a lamp. Or her nose.

"Are you all right?" Troy crouched next to her, touching her bare shoulder.

"Maybe I'm looking for something under the bed," she muttered as she glanced up at him, hoping she was still asleep and this was just another bad dream.

He cast a leisurely look down her naked back, grinning as he frankly perused her ass. "Perhaps your underwear?"

"I don't wear them," she snapped. Grabbing a sheet from the bed, she tugged it down and wrapped it around herself as she stood up. "Didn't you get enough of seeing me naked last night?"

He shook his head. "Is that a trick question?" Continuing to stare her up and down, he murmured, "You know, like asking a woman if she can ever own enough shoes? She might try to lie, so she doesn't look greedy, but deep in her heart, she's dying for one more pair of Prada's."

Considering Venus was a shoe woman all the way, she found the comparison immensely flattering. "What do you want?" she asked.

She looked him over as she waited for his reply. He wasn't dressed for work. He wore a pair of gym shorts and a sleeveless muscle shirt, which should have looked out of place on Mr. V.P., but instead looked damned sinful. He'd either just showered or gone swimming. His body glistened with a sheen of moisture that accented the rippling muscles of his arms and chest.

Perfect. Here she was with hair flying in twenty directions, a serious case of morning breath and probably a fat lip where her face had hit the floor.

Femme fatales worldwide must be quivering in mortification.

"You're a little accident prone, aren't you? Remind me to never let you drive my car."

"No. I absolutely am not," she retorted, holding the

sheet against her chest while she ran her other hand through her hair, trying to smooth it down. "And, besides, I don't like your car."

His eyes widened in disbelief. "Okay, that's going too far. You just insulted my Jag."

Men and cars. Who could figure? "It's too small," she explained. "Or I'm too tall. We just don't fit well together."

Now, there was an understatement. She fit in with his car about as well as she fit in with this man or with this house.

That'd be a big fat zero percent.

"It's a convertible. I can put the top down."

"Wouldn't that do wonders for my hair?"

He cast a doubtful look at her head. "Oh, yes, that would be a tragedy."

Venus thought about letting go of the sheet long enough to punch him in the gut, but figured the sheet would fall and he'd get yet another chance to see her stark naked and vulnerable. "Exactly what is it you want?"

"What size are you? Ten? Twelve?"

"Excuse me?"

Instead of answering, he walked around her, studying her head to toe. "Probably a ten...but with those hips..."

"I'm a perfect eight," she snarled, wondering how her day had gone from so-so to lousy in a two-minute time span.

He snickered. "Yeah. Right. Okay, have a good day." Then he turned toward the door.

She grabbed his arm, almost tripping on the sheet tangled around her feet. "Why do you want to know my size?"

He paused, smiling gently. "You went to bed so early

last night, you didn't get a chance to hear Max's plans. He wants to take us to some charity dinner at the country club tomorrow."

Though Venus hadn't eaten much the previous night, she suddenly felt as if she had a full stomach. A full stomach on a roller-coaster ride. She raised a shaky hand to her lips. "His country club?"

He seemed to see her nervousness immediately. "It's all right, Venus. I'll make sure you have something to wear."

"All the better to spill on, my dear?"

He stepped closer, pushing her wildly curling hair off her face with a touch so tender she almost sighed. "You'll be fine. We'll talk tonight, okay? And we'll get you ready."

"Ready to enjoy eating cold soup and meat with a pulse? I doubt it," she said as she flopped on to the bed, lying on her back. She stared at the ceiling. "I want to go home."

"Home is better than designer clothes and country clubs?" he asked, sitting beside her on the bed, taking her hand but making no attempt to move too close.

She somehow doubted the role of comforter came naturally to the man, but he was pretty darn good at it, anyway. "Home is beer and pizza. Laughter at Flanagan's, my uncle's pub. Games of darts. Betting on the Orioles." Still lying next to him on the huge bed, she turned to stare at him. "What's home to you?"

"Sales circulars," he murmured. "Meetings. New lines." He chuckled lightly. "Battles with my grandmother about the suitability of the date I brought to the last holiday party."

"That sounds interesting."

He glanced at her out the corner of his eye and admitted, "My grandmother doesn't seem to approve of my taste in women."

"Oh?" she asked, trying to hide her keen interest. "You have a certain type you like?"

He laughed softly. "The breathing type."

She slowly rose on the bed until she sat next to him. "Are you trying to tell me you're a dog?"

He narrowed his eyes, obviously thinking about it. Then, slowly, he nodded. "I suppose that's as accurate as anything."

"I don't believe it." She crossed her arms in front of her chest, careful not to dislodge the sheet, and gave him a look of pure skepticism. "Dogs don't admit they're dogs."

He shrugged. "Ex-dog? Reformed dog?"

"Neutered dog?" she said with a wicked grin.

He raised a brow, daring her to remember how totally bogus that claim was. She giggled, saying, "Okay, that one's out."

"I should say so."

Though it was early in the morning, and she was in a strange house, having a conversation with a man she'd known less than a day—and, oh, yeah, almost naked— Venus wanted to know more. "So does the respectable, conservative, suit-wearing businessman by day live a double life?"

He took a moment before answering. Then, finally, he sighed. "I guess I did, though I didn't really see it at the time. Trent is convinced my romantic troubles came about as a result of having to be the good twin growing up."

She raised a dubious brow, remembering the naked man who'd made no effort to grab for the towel yesterday afternoon. "You're the good twin? Lordy, I think I wanna meet your brother."

"I said growing up," he clarified. "We switched roles somewhere along the line. He's now settled down, happily married and soon to become a father."

"But it wasn't always like that?"

"No. Trent used to be the one in trouble for skipping school. The one who wrecked cars as a teenager. He took up every dangerous sport there is—skydiving, mountain climbing, street racing."

She began to understand. While she'd always thought it would be kinda cool having a twin, she now saw the flip side. Imagine being pressured from a young age to be the opposite of a person who physically looked just like you? "And you were the good son, great student, the suck-up rich kid who was supposed to honor the family name and make dad proud, right?"

He shifted on the bed, turning to face her. "Suck up? You've got the most colorful vocabulary."

She ignored him. "So Trent was the troubled teen, while by day you lived your dutiful, assigned role, and by night..."

He shrugged. "I snuck women into my room."

Sounded like her kind of guy. Too bad she'd already decided she couldn't have him. Now, though, sitting in her rumpled bed, still lethargic and warm from her sheets, she could hardly remember *why* she couldn't have him. "I suppose your brother's theory makes sense, and it could be part of what's driven you...."

"But?" he asked, looking very interested in her opinion. More interested than she'd have expected.

"But isn't it possible, Troy, that, uh, you also just really...like sex?"

He started to laugh, genuinely amused. "Yeah. That's

what I always figured," he admitted. "How funny someone I've known for less than a day would understand."
His laughter gradually faded and he simply looked at her
face. He studied her intently and repeated, "How
funny."

"Maybe I understand it because I'm a lot like you," she
admitted softly. "There's plenty of stuff in the world that
can stress me out or bring me down. Should I feel
ashamed because sex isn't one of them?"

He instantly reminded her of their conversation the
night before. "Then why has it been since last fall for
you?"

She answered his question with a question of her own.
"Well, why are you now 'reformed'?"

They stared at each other, both realizing the conversation had somehow gotten more intense and personal
than they'd ever intended. Certainly it had on Venus's
part. She had no problem talking to this mouthwatering
man about sex. But about silly things like family and babies and a fast-approaching thirtieth birthday? He didn't
need to hear about how she'd awakened one day and decided she wanted real emotion and commitment for the
first time in her life. He'd probably laugh in her face.

"All I can say," he replied, "is that if we'd met a year
ago, we wouldn't be sitting here just *talking* right now."

His mouth curved into a knowing smile, and all Venus
could think about was the way he'd tasted when they'd
kissed. She focused on a bead of sweat on his jaw, which
drew her attention to the strong beat of his pulse in his
neck. His skin would taste salty right there, his heart
would beat hard against her if she fell back onto the bed
and pulled him down on top of her.

When he met her eyes, his expression told her he knew
exactly what she was feeling, and felt the same.

No. They wouldn't be talking. They'd be all over each other. She wasn't fool enough to try denying it even to herself.

"We'd be...."

"Yeah," he said with complete certainty. "We would."

She nervously licked her lips, wincing slightly as she touched her tongue to a tender, swollen spot. He leaned closer, close enough that she could feel his breath on the side of her face. Then he gently touched his mouth to hers, delicately licking the sore spot.

"You're gonna have a fat lip," he murmured as he teased her with incredibly light touches of his tongue.

She moaned deep in her throat. "Are you kissing it to make it better?" She shifted on the bed to face him more fully.

"Uh-huh. Is it helping?"

No. Not helping. He might be making her mouth feel better, but other body parts were beginning to feel distinctly uncomfortable. Needy. Hot. "I might have bumped myself in one or two other places, too."

He laughed softly. "I'd love to kiss all of those places and make them feel better, Venus." Then, he reluctantly pulled away. "But I guess I should get out of here. Because if I start, I'm not going to be able to stop."

For the rest of the day? Or forever? He pulled away before she could ask him to clarify.

Finally, in a shaky voice, she said, "Okay, size ten. Twelve if it's cut narrow in the hips and bust."

He smiled slowly as he rose to leave the room. "I'll see you tonight, Venus."

AS HE DROVE through downtown traffic on the way to the office, Troy dialed his brother's home number on his cell phone. Trent would probably be long gone, of course. No doubt he'd been up with the sun, out digging holes in the dirt, planting trees and mucking around in fertilizer. *Lovely.*

He'd often wondered where Trent got that earthy streak, Not that Troy disliked being outdoors. As a matter of fact, so far the one thing he hated about life in Atlanta was losing out on his mornings on the beach. In Florida he'd started every day with a run, watching the sunrise, enjoying those quiet, silent moments, disturbed only by the never-ending churning of the surf and the lonely calls of gulls and osprey. Here, he had to run down winding roads in the elite community where Max lived. Still beautiful scenery, if he counted mansions and BMW's. But not the same, not at all.

When his sister-in-law answered, he couldn't help flirting. She'd expect nothing less. "Hey beautiful, ready to leave that dog-faced gardener you're married to yet?"

She sighed. "What can I say? I've grown rather attached to those rough, calloused hands, even if he's not much to look at."

"How's my niece or nephew?"

"No longer making me throw up every morning, at least," Chloe responded. "This is awfully early for a social call."

He quickly explained what he wanted her to do. Since Chloe now worked full-time in management at the store, having finished up her education last year shortly after she and Trent had married, she was the perfect person to ask. "And don't say anything to anyone else, please. Just charge it to my account."

"Are you going to tell me why you need this stuff? Or should I use my imagination?"

"Let's say I'm helping a friend prepare for an elegant dinner for Max tomorrow night."

She snorted. "Tell me you're not bringing a hooker to your boss's dinner."

He grinned, wondering what Venus would say to being called a hooker. Considering she was one of the least judgmental people he'd ever met, he doubted she'd be too offended. "No, actually this person might be a long-lost member of the family."

"Oh? As in long-lost distant cousin or something?"

"No. Possibly Max's granddaughter."

Chloe whistled, then zoned in on the key issue. "Max's granddaughter? Someone who could interfere with the merger?"

"You're too quick," he said as he cut down a side street to the parking lot of his building. "I think I liked you better when you were dressing windows."

"Even when you starred in them?" she quipped, referring to the display windows she'd done at Langtree's last summer, when she and Trent had met and she'd mistaken him for Troy. She'd been pretty obvious about her feelings, and the displays had reflected that.

A lifelong habit of intentionally trying to get under his more emotional brother's skin had made Troy intentionally pretend an interest in her, even though she'd really wanted Trent from the start. "Look, don't worry about it, Chloe. Max is still planning on going ahead with the deal. Venus is...a distraction, that's all. Even if she does turn out to be Max's granddaughter, I don't think she'd want any part of Longotti Lines."

He spoke the truth. He honestly didn't picture Venus having any desire to pick up and move to Atlanta to run her grandfather's company. She'd know better than anyone that she had no experience, no qualifications, and would be better off if Max sold out. The sale would bring a whole lot more cash into the family, which would no doubt seem beneficial to someone who might prove to be his main heir.

"Venus?" his sister-in-law asked doubtfully.

"I'm pulling into the parking lot right now. I'll talk to you later," he said, cutting the connection. He did not want to try to explain Venus to his sister-in-law. He didn't think he could do her justice, though he imagined Chloe would just love hearing about a woman who'd called him a snot to his face.

Venus was the kind of woman who had to be met in person to be appreciated. No way could he describe the way her aggressive attitude and smart-ass personality hid a vulnerable woman underneath. He shouldn't be so sure of that, not after such a short relationship, but he was. As much as she'd hate to admit it, Venus could be very easily hurt.

It would also be impossible for him to talk about her to Chloe without revealing some of the crazy feelings he had for the woman. Lust, well, that was a given. He'd been hot for Venus the moment he set eyes on her.

But he also liked her. He liked the way her brilliant green eyes glittered when she was angry. Liked the way she didn't back down to anyone—not him, not Max, not Leo. Liked her honest ability to talk about her own short-comings. Liked the fond way she spoke of her foster family. He liked that she didn't moan and groan about her situation, other than worrying about not fitting in. Liked the way she tried to act more tough when she was afraid or nervous.

Basically, he liked the way he felt when he was with her.

"Alive," he murmured. Alive and anticipatory, never quite knowing what she was going to do next, or how he'd react to it.

He'd never in his life felt like that with another woman.

Troy somehow managed to put Venus out of his thoughts for most of the work day. Still new to his job, he had a lot of reading to do, meetings with manufacturers and a union rep. Their telemarketing contract was up for renewal and he was charged with drawing up the short list of companies. And, of course, in the back of his mind during every decision was the constant thought about the potential merger.

As he packed up to leave at the end of the day, he asked Max's secretary if she needed him to bring anything home to the elder man. Max hadn't come in that day—he'd been busy entertaining his house guest. After bidding the woman and some of the other office staff good-night, he paused in Leo's doorway. The man's office was dark and empty, as it had been all day.

Obviously Leo had taken the day off, too. One of these days, Troy really did have to find out what the man did to earn his six-figure salary. Other than hover over Max, pushing pills in his hand and taking him to doctor's appointments.

As he exited the building and flicked the alarm button on his key chain, he glanced appraisingly at his car. The memory of Venus's words from this morning made him chuckle. "Sorry she doesn't like you, sweetheart."

A woman who flat-out told him she didn't like his car—that was a first. And almost as bad, in Troy's opinion, as telling a man he wasn't good in bed, or had a little... He shuddered.

Troy had certainly never been told either of those things. Uh-uh. Never in a million years. But the car comment had definitely stung, almost as much as it had amused him. Particularly because of the adorable way she'd looked wrapped up in the silky sheets, all rumpled and warm from her bed when she'd said it. And the way she'd looked flat on her face on the floor, bare-ass naked when he'd entered her room.

"That was pretty good too," he said with a nod as he unlocked the car.

He wondered where Max and Venus had spent their day. Last night, before the unfortunate choking incident, Max had offered to take Venus to one of the premier shopping complexes nearby. The center was filled with exclusive stores including Sak's and Cartier, that should, ideally, make any con woman's eyes light up with anticipation.

She'd instead told Max she preferred to visit Margaret Mitchell's house.

He wouldn't have pegged Venus for a big southern romance nut. Then again, maybe she saw something of herself in Scarlett O'Hara. He had the feeling Venus fancied herself a man-eater, a hard, ruthless seductress. Maybe some other people pictured her that way, too.

"Wrong." Troy shook his head ruefully as he started the car and drove out of the parking lot.

As far as he was concerned, Venus was as ruthless as a kitten. Sure, she exuded confidence and brazen sex appeal. Yeah, she had guts. Certainly she'd done something most women wouldn't have had the nerve to do... dropping that towel yesterday.

He took a moment to appreciate the mental picture.

Still, underneath it all was a sensitive woman who, he believed, wouldn't hurt anybody intentionally. How he could be so sure, he couldn't say. Intuition? Years of experience with so many women he'd come to understand the sex? Maybe even a little wishful thinking? All of the above?

He didn't know for sure, but he truly believed it.

Troy wasn't fool enough to completely rule out the possibility of Venus being involved in some kind of scheme with Leo Gallagher. But he would bet that if it came down to actually hurting somebody, she would never go through with it.

He just hoped she didn't prove him wrong.

When he arrived back at the house, he immediately looked around for Max and Venus. Following the sound of laughter into the entertainment room, as Max called it, he stopped in the doorway to look at them.

Venus and Max were sitting opposite one another over a huge coffee table, trying to bounce coins into a mug of beer. Max's face was tight with concentration as he focused on flipping his wrist just so to get the quarter to land in the mug. "Ah-ha!" the man cried when he was successful.

"See?" Venus said with a triumphant grin. "It's all in the angle of your fingers."

"Drink," Max ordered.

Shaking his head ruefully, Troy entered the room. "I haven't played quarters since my frat house days."

Venus glanced at him out of the corner of her eye. "Oh, do they play such low drinking games at the University for the Uptight and Pretentious?"

Max snickered.

"Nice to see you too," Troy replied. "Have a good time on your shopping trip?" He cast a long, studying glance over her tight jeans and tank top. "I see you didn't shop for clothes."

She stood and struck a provocative pose, fisting her hand and putting it on one jean-clad hip. The jeans fit her like a second skin, drawing attention to her long, slim legs and the curve of her rear. The cotton top was also wickedly tight and was low cut enough for him to see the tops of her lush breasts and a tempting hint of cleavage. "You don't like my clothes, Troy? Aww, that hurts my feelings."

As she intended, her exaggerated pout looked sultry and inviting, reminding him of the way they'd kissed. He swallowed, trying not to let her see how she so easily affected him. The look of triumph in her eyes told him he'd failed. This was definitely not a woman to whom he wanted to give the upper hand. She was quite used to walking all over men—but, Troy wasn't like most other men. He'd done some walking of his own.

"We didn't go shopping," Max explained, the twinkle in his eye negating his grudging tone. "Venus dragged me to that writer's house, then we went to have lunch at a terribly touristy restaurant called Melissa's Tap Room."

"'That writer,'" Venus muttered in disgust. "And it was *Melanie's* Tea Room." She turned to Troy. "Can you believe this man has lived in Atlanta for seventy years and has never seen or read *Gone With The Wind?*"

"Sacrilege," Troy mumbled as he loosened his tie.

Venus nodded, not acknowledging his sarcasm. "I mean, imagine, living in Atlanta where it all took place— while you were living here—and not seeing it!"

Max tilted his head and raised a brow, obviously trying to look insulted. "I know you told me this morning I'm...how did you put it? Older than dirt? But I must say I'm offended you think I'm old enough to have been around for the war between the states."

She rolled her eyes. "I didn't mean the actual war. I meant the movie release, the big premiere, all that stuff."

"Older than dirt?" Troy asked, again amazed at the easy camaraderie between the pair.

Venus grimaced. "The man has Liberace CDs in his car."

"Oh, that certainly explains it," Troy said. "Two strikes, Max. Liberace and a *Gone With The Wind* virgin."

"But not for long," Venus replied with a Cheshire cat smile as she sat back down.

Almost afraid to ask, Troy glanced at Max. The older man let out an exaggerated sigh. "We stopped and bought a copy."

"We waited to order the pizza until you got here."

"Pizza?" Troy asked, hearing her merriment.

Venus grinned. "If Max is going to drag me into his club tomorrow night and a fancy party Friday, he can do something I want to do tonight."

Pizza, beer and a video. Sounded good to Troy, especially after his long day, though he would never have chosen the mother of all chick flicks. "All right, do I have time to change?"

She nodded. "Grab a box of tissues before you come back." She told Max, "This is a real tearjerker, with a killer ending."

"If you ruin the ending of the movie, young lady, you can forget this idea right now," Max replied tartly. "That's as bad as people who read the end of a book first."

Venus looked at her own hands. "Uh, guilty."

Max's eyes widened in horror. "No."

"Well, what's the point of reading a whole book if it's going to have a sucky ending?"

"There's such a thing as the journey," Max said. "Oh, dear, I see I'm going to have to introduce you to some books worth reading simply for the sake of the words."

Venus snorted. "Great words can't make me like a book." She glanced at Troy through lowered lashes.

"Though if it's got some great sex or some bloody bodies or, better still, a bit of both, I might be interested."

Max shook his head in amusement. Tapping his finger on his cheek, he said, "I think I might have a few that would meet your requirements. And they might even have an ending you'd approve of." He gestured toward the DVD case. "Though the ending to this is so awful, I can't imagine why you insist we see it."

Troy hid a smile, liking the liveliness in Max's eye and his obvious good mood. The man looked ten years younger than he had last week. He had to give Venus credit for that—she could breathe life into any house.

"Ignore her, Max," he said as he turned to leave the room. "It's got a great ending."

"What do you mean, great?" Venus asked, looking highly annoyed. "It's tragic."

Max covered his ears and glared. "I'm not listening."

Troy grinned. "As far as I'm concerned," he said in a loud whisper, "it's a happily ever after. Any man who stayed with *her* would be completely insane within a month." Her eyes narrowed. Before she could reply, Troy said, "Back in a minute...Scarlett."

7

VENUS GLANCED at the clock yet again, noting it was nearly 1:00 a.m. Though she'd gone to bed over an hour before, she still felt wide-awake. She told herself her insomnia was a product of the pizza. She knew better, however.

Men, she decided, were usually the best reason to remain awake late into the night. But the man ruining her sleep this night wasn't in her bed, keeping her up with long, slow, erotic lovemaking that would curl her toes and leave her limp and sated. He was on the other side of the wall, probably sleeping peacefully, as comfortable and relaxed as a baby. Probably naked and warm, rumpled and ready.

She groaned.

Venus had wanted him terribly when they first met, and even more when she saw him naked—whoa, mama, had she wanted him when he was naked! But somehow it was the Troy she'd sat next to on the sofa tonight, drinking beer, licking cheesy pizza off his fingers, teasing her mercilessly about the schmaltzy sentimentality of the movie they were watching, who really had her too confused to sleep.

Damn. She enjoyed being with the man. How bizarre was that? Lust was one thing—she knew lust, she trusted lust. It was reliable and instinctive, easily assuaged. Or *usually* easily assuaged—just not in this case.

Play the Romance Crossword Game

and get...
2 FREE BOOKS

and a
FREE GIFT...

YOURS to KEEP!

Scratch Here!

to reveal the hidden words.
Look below to see what you get.

Yes!

I have scratched off the gold areas. Please send me my **2 FREE BOOKS** and **FREE GIFT** for which I qualify. I understand that I am under no obligation to purchase any books as explained on the back of this card.

▶ DETACH AND MAIL CARD TODAY! ▶

342 HDL DRT2

142 HDL DRUJ

FIRST NAME

LAST NAME

ADDRESS

APT.#

CITY

Visit us online at
www.eHarlequin.com

STATE/PROV.

ZIP/POSTAL CODE

ROMANCE	MYSTERY	NOVEL	GIFT
You get **2 FREE BOOKS** PLUS a **FREE GIFT!**	You get **2 FREE BOOKS!**	You get **1 FREE BOOK!**	You get a **FREE MYSTERY GIFT!**

The Harlequin Reader Service® — Here's how it works:

Accepting your 2 free books and mystery gift places you under no obligation to buy anything. You may keep the books and gift and return the shipping statement marked "cancel." If you do not cancel, about a month later we'll send you 4 additional books and bill you just $3.57 each in the U.S., or $4.24 each in Canada, plus 25¢ shipping & handling per book and applicable taxes if any.* That's the complete price and — compared to cover prices of $4.25 each in the U.S. and $4.99 each in Canada — it's quite a bargain! You may cancel at any time, but if you choose to continue, every month we'll send you 4 more books, which you may either purchase at the discount price or return to us and cancel your subscription.

*Terms and prices subject to change without notice. Sales tax applicable in N.Y. Canadian residents will be charged applicable provincial taxes and GST. Credit or Debit balances in a customer's account(s) may be offset by any other outstanding balance owed by or to the customer

If offer card is missing write to: Harlequin Reader Service, 3010 Walden Ave., P.O. Box 1867, Buffalo NY 14240-1867

BUSINESS REPLY MAIL
FIRST-CLASS MAIL   PERMIT NO. 717-003   BUFFALO, NY

POSTAGE WILL BE PAID BY ADDRESSEE

HARLEQUIN READER SERVICE
3010 WALDEN AVE
PO BOX 1867
BUFFALO NY 14240-9952

NO POSTAGE
NECESSARY
IF MAILED
IN THE
UNITED STATES

But liking? A man she enjoyed being around for the sheer pleasure of seeing the sparkle in his eyes when she baited him? For the sheer joy of exchanging sassy barbs? She'd only ever *liked* one other man with whom she'd been involved. Raul, and that hadn't ended well. She'd pulled back as soon as she started liking him too much, knowing they had no future and she could get hurt if they continued.

There was even less of a chance of anything lasting happening between her and Troy Langtree. Sure, he wanted her. Sure, she amused him. But as for anything long-term? Impossible. He was not only in a different social stratosphere, he'd also readily admitted to being a dog when it came to women. Temporarily reformed or not, she didn't imagine he was ever going to be the type to settle down to just one.

Besides, with Troy, having to pull back wasn't even an issue, since they weren't really involved. Well, unless she counted their few kisses, and the shattering orgasm he'd given her. "Don't start thinking about that," she told herself.

She glared at the clock, trying to push the picture of Troy Langtree out of her mind, desperate to think of something else.

Unfortunately, her thoughts easily segued to someone equally troubling to her peace of mind. Max—another man she'd never expected to like. But she did. She really liked the old guy, with his keen sense of humor—almost as wicked as her own. During the hours they'd spent together today, he'd teased her, instructed her, even joined her in pure cattiness on occasion, particularly when it came to anyone he deemed "too big for their britches."

Max really had a dislike for condescending people. Probably explained why Leo made his teeth hurt. It was funny that he liked Troy so much. Troy, however, wasn't so much arrogant as he was confident. And in spite of his occasional haughtiness, he'd never been condescending toward her—even when he'd practically accused her of being a con artist.

He hadn't mentioned it once today, and she wondered if he'd let go of his suspicions. She hoped so. For some reason she really didn't want the man to think badly of her. And she hoped he never found out she'd taken money from Leo to come on this trip, no matter how good her reasons had been.

Now, having spent some time with Max, she had to wonder if those reasons had been good enough. "Hell, yes, they were good enough," she muttered, tamping down any uncertainty and aiming for practicality instead. Max would be the first one to say keeping a roof over her own head and helping her foster family out were good enough reasons to take money from a weasel.

She didn't, however, know that Troy would agree. Max was a much more pragmatic man than Troy. Perhaps because he'd suffered a lot of loss in his life. That made as much sense as anything, mainly because Venus felt pretty much the same way about herself.

In any case, it hadn't made him bitter, and it hadn't made him self-pitying. Instead it had made him understanding. He'd also proven to be very interested in the people around him.

Today, he'd asked her about her childhood, seeming to enjoy hearing about what an unholy terror she'd been as a kid. He'd demanded to know her favorite foods, and whether she liked roller coasters. He'd asked her about her first date...and said he was going to put a hit out on Tony Cabrini for never calling her again after relieving her of her virginity in the laundry room.

She still couldn't believe she'd told that story to a seventy-something-year-old man. Max, she had to admit, was incredibly easy to talk to, and completely nonjudgmental.

Most importantly, he seemed to respect her unspoken desire to avoid talking about his late son. It was as if Max knew Venus was poised to bail, ready to head back to Baltimore if things got too hairy. Confronting her about the man who could be her father might be enough to put her feet in motion.

Max had somehow understood without being told. He'd been content to spend the day with her, getting to know her, enjoying her company like any two people who'd just met and believed they might have a few things in common worth exploring. Aside from that little bit of reminiscing the first evening, he hadn't brought up his son at all.

She looked at the clock again. A whopping three minutes since the last time she'd checked. Finally realizing there was no way she was going to be able to fall asleep, she decided to go for the swim she hadn't taken that morning. Sure it was late—one in the morning—but Max had said the pool was heated. And he'd said she was welcome to use it at any time.

Not turning on a light in her room, she pulled her swimsuit out of her suitcase and quickly donned it. She grabbed a towel out of the bathroom and silently made her way through the house, pausing only briefly outside Troy's bedroom door.

Silence. He was probably happily dreaming about boatloads of money and lots of willing women. She wondered what he'd think if one slipped into his room right now.

Enough.

She made her way through the big house, finding her way through the downstairs with the low lighting left on by the housekeeper, who'd watched the last hour of the movie with them.

She grinned when she remembered it. Max and Troy had applauded Rhett, while Venus and Mrs. Harris had haughtily informed them that he would be back.

"He should have married the other one," Max had said. "The nice one."

Venus had been unable to prevent a snort. "Oh, please. That's such a crock. Just like those old-fashioned romance novels."

Troy had smiled. "I'm sorry to admit I haven't read one lately. Do enlighten us."

"There was always a wicked hero reformed by the love of a sweet, virginal ingenue who wouldn't say crap if she stepped in it."

Max had grabbed his handkerchief to cover his laughter. Troy had simply waited.

"And he always chose the sweet nitwit over the evil wicked other woman who was horrible enough to admit she liked sex and had a brain in her head."

Troy had given her a knowing look. "You're saying opposites might attract, but they don't stay together?"

"Exactly."

"So two wicked people are a better match?" Max had interjected, looking back and forth between Venus and Troy as if aware of the undercurrents flowing between them.

"Absolutely." Venus had practically dared Troy to deny it.

"Even if she—how did I hear Troy put it when I didn't cover my ears enough?—drives him completely insane within a month?"

This time Troy had answered, his eyes never leaving

Venus's, holding her stare until she'd felt a little dizzy. "But, Max, I didn't mean it. They were perfect together. Because insanity is better than boredom any day."

Now, slipping quietly through the sun room to the French doors, Venus though about Troy's comment. She agreed. Insanity was way better than boredom. But she suspected Troy had simply been flirting with her and hadn't really meant what he'd said.

As she walked out the back door, her eyes quickly adjusted to the near darkness. Small garden lanterns illuminated the shrub-lined patio surrounding the huge free-form-shaped pool. The bright moon added its glow to light her way.

Still, it was almost dark enough that she didn't see the man in the water until she'd reached the steps.

She heard the splash first. Freezing where she stood, Venus scanned the pool and was finally able to make out the body slicing through the water. Strong arms and shoulders lifted in a steady rhythm. Thickly muscled legs kicked efficiently as the swimmer steadily traversed the length of the pool and back. Even before she recognized the wet, dark hair and the unmistakable body, she knew who it was. Troy.

A quick burst of doubt urged her to go back inside, knowing this might well be a very dangerous situation. Every time the two of them were together, sparks flew. Even clothed, in public, in daylight, they couldn't resist any opportunity to dance around the attraction so thick between them it could be spread on toast.

Now, late at night, half clothed, completely alone...it would be pure temptation. Definite danger.

Play it safe for a change and get out of here. Now.

But she couldn't. Instead, she stood there, watching the way his body moved, wondering how a man could look so masculine when doing something as basic as exercising.

Finally, after a few long, voyeuristic minutes, she watched as he paused for a breath at the ladder beside her feet. That's when he saw her. He was nearly concealed in the water, but she could see the way his chest heaved with deeply inhaled breaths as he watched her. His eyes glittering in the moonlight, he looked her over, from head to toe, his stare deliberate and appreciative.

She still held the towel in the tips of her fingers but it did nothing to cover her body, clothed, only in the most basic sense of the word, by the skimpy, royal blue bikini.

He looked his fill, then finally murmured, "Hello, Venus."

"Hi."

"We both had the same idea, I see."

She nodded. "I didn't know you were out here." Then, swallowing, she said, "Do you want me...to leave?"

"I want you...to do whatever it is you'd like to do," he responded, his pause every bit as provocative as hers had been.

She dropped the towel and stepped down one rung on the ladder, sighing at the feel of the water on her feet. "Warm."

"Very. I love swimming at night," he admitted, looking at the flecks of moonlight shimmering on the surface of the pool. "I do this a lot at the beach at home."

Still holding the rails for balance, and still facing him, she stepped down again, until the water reached her knees. "Night swimming in the ocean. Sounds a little too much like a blatant invitation to an all-you-can-eat buffet for any great white creatures swimming around down there."

He laughed softly. "Actually, I think I'm more afraid of

jellyfish." Then a look of pure devilment widened his smile. "Especially because I like to swim naked."

In the process of stepping to the third rung, she froze and stared at him. Her eyes shifted and she glanced at the water, trying to see beneath the dark surface. "You're, uh..."

"What?

"You like to swim naked?"

"Nothing feels better," he assured her. His voice was low and sultry, as smooth and silky as the fabric of her bikini.

She raised a brow. "Nothing?"

"Well, one or two things," he admitted with a soft chuckle. "But there aren't a whole lot of physical sensations that can compare to the feel of liquid warmth against your bare skin."

Parting her lips, she drew in a shaky breath, fully grasping his underlying meaning. She knew exactly what liquid warmth a man wanted against certain bare skin. Considering she got wet just looking at the man, she didn't think that would be a problem.

"Don't tell me bad, bad Venus has never skinny-dipped?"

She hadn't, not that she'd admit it. "You think I won't?"

He only answered with a tiny shrug as he put his head back and looked up at the star-filled sky. When he straightened, he swiped a lazy hand through his wet hair. Long streams of water glittered against his tanned skin, highlighting the corded muscles of his arm and shoulder as he moved. Another rush of pure desire spread through Venus's veins, warming her, making her even more achy and aware with every breath she took.

It really shouldn't be legal for a man to look so good.

"Coming?" He swam away from the wall in an easy backstroke.

As usual, when challenged, Venus reacted with bravado and instinct. Once she was sure she had Troy's full attention, she sat down on the top rung of the ladder, nearly cooing at the pleasure of the water against her thighs and bottom. Not saying another word, she reached around her back, feeling for the tie of her bathing suit top. She undid it slowly, so intent and focused, she could almost hear the wisp of the material as the strings gave way. Then she dropped her hand, feeling the warm night air brush against the bottom curves of her partially uncovered breasts.

Troy watched from a few feet away, never taking his eyes off her. He didn't urge her on, or try to stop her. He simply waited, more patient—more *confident*—than any man she'd ever known.

Giving him a sultry smile, she reached for the string at the back of her neck. Neither of them blinked. Venus hardly even breathed as she carefully untied the fastening. Then she let the top fall off her body, into her lap.

Though his only reaction was a slight widening of his eyes and a parting of his lips, Venus knew he liked what he saw. He couldn't take his gaze off her.

Feeling very wanton, and very sure of her own power as a woman, Venus dipped her cupped hand into the water. She slowly raised it to her throat, pouring a trail of liquid down the front of her body. Sighing at the cool relief against her heated skin, she closed her eyes to savor the sensation.

A moment later, she reached in and drew up another handful. Again, she gently poured it on her body, focusing on the pleasure of it as the gentle droplets slid down her throat, across her collarbone, then over the curve of her breast.

A drop of water reached her puckered nipple and hung there, practically inviting him to come taste it. She wanted more than anything for him to lick the drop off her, to warm her cool skin with the heat of his mouth, to take her nipple between his lips and suck deeply on her flesh.

He swam closer, silently, cutting expertly through the water. His piercing stare never left her body. And almost before she'd fully realized what she'd started, he was there, holding on to the rails on either side of her. He stayed below her, one rung down, his chest between her parted thighs.

"You're wet," he murmured. Then, as if he simply couldn't help himself, he leaned close and licked away a bit of moisture in the hollow of her throat.

She moaned. "Troy."

He ignored her protest. Or maybe it was a plea. She couldn't think straight enough to decide.

"I didn't get it all yet." He followed the trail of the water, his tongue and warm breaths sending a path of pure fire across her skin. She didn't move, could only clutch the metal handrails, her fingers close to his, so close, but not touching. Just his mouth. His tongue. On her chest. Until, finally, his lips were at the curve of her breast. She whimpered as he moved lower. Then, finally, he licked the single drop of water from her nipple with one slow, deliberate flick of his tongue.

She almost came right there on the step.

"Thank you," he said. Then, with a sultry smile, he extended his arms behind him and leisurely swam away.

Venus watched, slack-jawed, ready to order him to get back over here and finish what he'd started. He paused a yard or so from the side of the pool, treading water again. Watching her, he waited for her next move, as if he'd lobbed the ball back on her side of the court and wanted to see if she had the guts to hurl it back toward him.

Not about to let him think he'd nearly shattered her with his much-too-brief caress, Venus moved her hand down her body, following the path his lips had taken. She paused for a fleeting moment as her fingers reached her nipple, moving it as lightly and deftly as he had moved his tongue. She knew he understood she was mimicking what he'd done.

She felt sure she heard a tiny groan, but supposed it could have been the breeze blowing through the branches of a tree.

Then she lowered her hand under the water. Standing on the last rung, she bent and pushed the bathing suit bottoms off. Naked, she tossed both pieces of wet material to the pool deck.

"You're right," she whispered as she felt the liquid sluicing between her thighs, cooling her where she was most hot. "This feels amazing."

Submerging completely beneath the surface, she kicked off the wall and swam for several yards, toward the shallow end of the pool. The feeling of being naked, enveloped by warm, gentle water, was incredibly sensual. She'd never felt more free while swimming and loved the way her body slid so intimately through the surrounding wetness.

When she finally came up for breath, she found herself standing in thigh-deep water. She made no effort to go deeper, or to cover herself. She wanted him to look at her. Wanted him to want her every bit as much as she wanted him.

Troy surfaced a few feet away, concealed from the waist down. "Venus rising from the waves," he said. She saw his breaths deepen as he studied her, his gaze lingering on the curve of her throat, then her breasts. He looked lower, to her waist and hips, then at the shadowed curls between her thighs brushing lightly, with delicious sensitivity, against the surface of the pool.

"You do look beautiful." His voice was thick, revealing his reaction to her. "As wanton and desirable as any goddess of love should look."

He approached her. She held her breath and made no effort to move away. Then, as his body emerged, she noticed a band of black fabric around his hips. She couldn't prevent a tiny laugh, knowing she'd been tricked. "You're wearing trunks."

He shrugged, completely unrepentant. "I never said I wasn't."

"So why did you dare me to take off my suit?"

"I didn't dare you, Venus," he replied with a knowing smile. He moved closer, until they stood only inches apart. "You are perfectly capable of doing whatever you want to do, whenever you want to do it."

True...except when it came to him. Because what she really wanted to do was reach out and tug that suit off him, to see if he was as aroused and ready as he'd been in the bathroom. As she was right now. Then she wanted to wrap her legs around him and let their bodies move together in the gentle flow of the water.

He continued. "Do you blame me for understanding you well enough to know you'd take off your clothes and swim gloriously naked in the moonlight if given the slightest provocation?"

She shook her head, tsking. "You didn't even try to stop me, when you knew what I thought."

Lowering his gaze to her bare breasts, he whispered, "What kind of fool would do that?"

Making a split-second decision, she reached for the waistband of his trunks. "Maybe the same kind of fool who would have handed you the towel in the bathroom?"

He laughed softly.

"Or the kind of fool who *wouldn't* insist turnabout is fair play," she murmured, determined to even the stakes.

Troy had only intended to tease her a little, to taunt Venus into doing exactly what she'd done. He had no compunction about tricking her into removing her clothes. After all, he'd been remembering her naked ever since the moment she'd dropped the towel in the bathroom. He'd wanted to look at her stunning body again almost as much as he wanted to lose himself in it.

He hadn't, however, counted on being completely unable to control his reaction. He'd managed to back away after one quick self-indulgent taste of her supple skin.

He'd tried to keep his desire for her in check, not wanting her to see the intense storm of need almost making him shake. But when she reached for him, when she brushed the tips of her fingers against his stomach in a long, slow caress, he couldn't prevent a deep groan.

"Oh," she whispered, obviously hearing his need and seeing the coiled tightness of his body. "You're not quite as unaffected as you wanted me to think, are you?"

He shook his head, unable to lie about something so damned obvious. "No." He slipped his hand into her hair, tangling his fingers in the wet strands. "Venus, I've wanted you since the minute I laid eyes on you."

She moved her cool fingers lower and grasped the waistband of his suit. He leaned closer, making it easier for her to remove the trunks.

"That's your answer?" she asked, apparently recognizing the move for the confirmation it was.

"Yes."

She didn't hesitate, not that he'd expected her to. Troy waited, watching her nibble the corner of her lips as she pushed the suit down his hips until he could kick them off under the water. He hissed when she cupped his ass, squeezing him tightly, pulling him closer. His wet erection slid against her bare stomach, making them both quiver.

"So we do this, we do what we've wanted to do since the minute we met, we, uh, get it out of our systems, and that's the end of it?" she asked as she slipped her arms around his neck and pulled him closer for a kiss.

He chuckled, truly amused. "Hell, no, Venus." He gently tugged her head back, still cupping it, still stroking her hair, touching her soft earlobe, scraping his fingertip along her nape. Her green eyes were wide and excited, full of anticipation as she met his stare.

"We do this," he told her, pressing his body suggestively against hers in an instinctive male question that she answered silently with a feminine thrust of her hips. "And then we do it again." He kissed her temple. "And again." Moving lower, he lightly nipped her earlobe. "And again." After sampling her neck, he moved his way to her mouth.

Just before their lips touched, she gave a helpless groan and whispered, "Works for me."

Then he was kissing her deeply, tasting her, feeling her warmth and acceptance. Their tongues danced and mated as she melted against him, her naked body warm and vibrant. The scrape of her pointed nipples against his chest nearly made him lose his mind as her hands stroked his back and then her nails dug into his shoulders.

"Do you know how crazy it's been making me, wanting to touch you like this?" he whispered when they parted for breath, hearing the hoarse need in his voice that he couldn't possibly disguise.

"Like this?" she asked, drawing his hand up to her breast, offering that perfect, puckered flesh to him.

He knew what she wanted as she pressed against his hand. Instead, he drew out the tension, moving his hand away to delicately rub her collarbone and the hollow of her throat. He built the fire, even though he knew it was already hot enough to burn them both up.

He should have known Venus wouldn't respond with similar restraint. She pushed him back until he lost his footing and almost fell under the water. When he rose again, she kissed the surprised laughter off his lips. "No more teasing, Troy. I just can't take it," she said, making no effort to play coy.

She wanted what she wanted. And she wanted it now.

God, he loved a woman who didn't play games when it came to something as elemental as sex.

"Fine," he promised her. "No more teasing. But I reserve the right to some serious foreplay at a future date."

"Deal."

"By the way, I really *like* foreplay, Venus."

Venus heard a note of something in Troy's voice and saw his amusement segue to pure male drive. Before she realized what he intended, he'd picked her up by the hips and tugged her legs around his waist. The warmth of his erection slid between the wet folds of her body, coming close, so close to where she wanted him. Beginning to pant and quiver, she arched closer, trying to take what he wasn't yet giving her.

"Not yet," he muttered just before he lowered his mouth to her breast, as if he had to taste her, now, or die.

She jerked when he captured one sensitive nipple and sucked it deeply into his mouth—hard. Yes. *This* was what she wanted, what she'd demanded moments ago.

He completely supported her weight, easily holding her with one arm as she arched back invitingly. He thoroughly tasted both her breasts, nibbling and suckling one while he playfully stroked and cajoled the other with his fingers. She wriggled and writhed against him, not wanting him to stop, but wanting more than just his hands and mouth.

"Are you protected?" he asked raggedly, his tone telling her she'd damn well better be.

"Yes. The pill."

"Good."

Then, with one agonizingly perfect thrust, he plunged deep into her, filling her up until she cried out at the pleasure of it. He caught her cries with a wet kiss as they both absorbed the sensations. Hot bodies. Cool water. Deep... *deep* penetration.

She'd never felt anything more pleasurable in her life.

"This is just the first time, right?" she somehow managed to say, almost crying at how good he felt, so thick and solid inside her. "There's an again?"

"Absolutely." He cupped her head, pulling her close for more of those slow, hot kisses that completely melted her and made her want to devour him at the same time. "Several agains."

"Oh, thank heaven," she managed to whimper, needing him to move, faster, deeper, harder. "Then could you please, *please* go slow next time. Right now I want...I need..."

She didn't have to finish. He seemed suddenly as out of control as Venus, catching her around the waist and pounding into her with deep, soul-shattering thrusts. The water gushed against her in never-ending, undulating liquid caresses. His mouth licked hungrily at her own. He filled her so deeply she imagined she'd feel him inside her forever.

And finally, when he dropped his head back and shouted out his completion, he gave her another of those screaming orgasms.

8

LESS THAN TWO WEEKS on the job and he was going to be late for work. Troy glanced at his watch, seeing it was after nine, and hit the gas. He didn't imagine his new boss would care for his excuse. *Sorry, Max, I overslept because I was up until four having the most amazing sex of my life with your granddaughter. Man, we did things I didn't even know were possible.*

No, he didn't want to have to explain. Especially because he couldn't think about last night without getting hard again.

Venus. She'd been incredible. He'd never known a woman as completely in tune with her own body, and her lover's. They'd read each other's moods, known what each other wanted. When to slow down, or when to pound forward. Every touch had been savored, every stroke answered in return.

After that first frantic encounter in the pool, Trent had carried her out and gently dried her off. They'd curled up on a padded lounge chair, exchanging kisses and caresses for an hour as the night shadows deepened. More lovemaking, this time sweet and languorous, had followed.

They didn't come inside until almost three. After he'd placed her in bed, Venus had sleepily whispered, "When you mentioned those *agains*, did you mean all of them tonight?"

He'd chuckled and held her until she fell asleep. Then, not wanting to risk discovery in the morning, he'd left her warm bed and gone back to his own. As much as he'd wanted to say goodbye to her this morning, he hadn't gotten the chance. He'd call her from the office in a while, just to hear her voice. Of course, that sounded sappy as hell, so he'd have to pretend to be calling to see if his package had arrived.

Venus would know, anyway. The woman could read him better than anyone ever had.

While thinking of the package he was expecting today, he reached for his cell phone. Max had mentioned another event—a semiformal party—scheduled for Friday night. Venus would be no more prepared for that than she would for tonight's dinner at the club. He quickly dialed his brother's home number.

"This is starting to become a habit," Chloe said when he identified himself.

"I'm glad I caught you. I was afraid you might have left for the store already," he replied.

"Doctor's appointment." He heard a crunching sound and knew she was eating while holding the phone. Trent had told him Chloe had constant cravings for apples. He hoped his godchild liked them since that and Doritos were about all Chloe had sent down to the poor kid in the past several months.

"What's up?" she asked.

"Did you get the stuff for me?"

"Uh-huh. It'll be there by three."

"Great. I need another favor." He told her what he wanted.

She whistled. "Very nice. I've seen that dress and thought about using my employee's discount myself."

"I think you need to be shopping in another department," he teased.

"Yeah, the beached whale department," she said. "I swear to God, if the doctor's wrong and this is twins, I'm going to kill you and your brother."

"Whoa, I didn't have anything to do with it."

"Damn right you didn't." Trent's voice. He'd picked up on another extension.

"Aw, hell, why are you home?" Troy asked. "Shouldn't you be out pulling weeds or something?"

"I'm taking Chloe to the doctor." Then, as expected, his twin tossed an insult right back at him. "What about you? Sounds like you're stuck in traffic. Shouldn't you be sitting at a desk getting fat and pasty?"

"Oh, and Troy," Chloe said, ignoring the insults, "I nixed the stockings. The shoes you picked cry out for bare legs."

Venus with bare legs. That worked.

"Tall woman?" Chloe asked, quite obviously fishing.

"Yeah. How'd you know?"

"The shoe size. Is she a blonde?"

"Redhead."

She let out a long "ahh," which probably meant something to her, or to anyone with a uterus, but which he didn't get at all.

"Does this mean your self-imposed celibacy is over?" Trent asked. "And you're out of this miserable mood you've been in?"

He frowned. "I haven't been in a miserable mood."

"Yeah, you have," Chloe said. "Ever since that dingbat got you all tied up in knots because you asked her to lunch and didn't show up with a wedding ring."

Troy was so startled by Chloe's comment that he nearly cut off a semi loaded with beer in the next lane.

The driver laid on his horn, and Troy jerked the steering wheel. He gave the guy an apologetic wave and got flipped off in return.

"You there?"

"Sorry," he muttered. "Now, what are you talking about?"

"Oh, come on, Troy. You've been doing the self-flagellation thing for months. I could understand if you'd done anything to deserve it." She muttered something under her breath, which sounded suspiciously like *as usual*. "But this time you didn't. You took her out, it didn't work, and she got all whacked out about it. You just wanted to spend some time with someone you thought was 'nice'—for a change—and she turned out be a loony." She crunched her apple again while Troy thought it over. "What I don't get is why you went out with her in the first place," she mumbled between bites. "You must have caught some of my pregnancy hormones and temporarily lost your mind."

"They're catching?" he asked.

"Oh, yeah," Trent said. Troy had forgotten he was on the extension. "Women turn into goo-gooing know-it-alls who want to rub Chloe's stomach and tell her how to breast-feed."

He could definitely get into the breast thing, but that's about as far as he could relate.

"And men look at me like I should be strutting because the whole world knows I actually had sex with my wife at least once."

"Hopefully not in the store after hours," Troy said with a wicked chuckle, reminding them of one of their premarital dates.

"Trent Langtree, you are a dead man," Chloe said,

suddenly sounding incensed. "How could you tell him about that?"

Troy let his twin sweat and sputter for a minute. "I didn't say he told me." He heard Trent's relieved sigh, then decided to pay his brother back for the fat and pasty crack. "Maybe he just forgot to turn off one of the security cameras."

He hung up as Chloe shrieked, figuring he'd admit he'd lied later. Trent would never kiss and tell—he'd always played his romantic cards close to the chest. Troy had put two and two together when the security guard had admitted Trent had bribed him to leave them alone in the store one night last summer.

Picturing his twin trying to convince his wife of that, he laughed all the way to work. Damn, he really missed his brother.

When he arrived, the first thing Troy took care of was a quick call to the rental office of his new apartment building. They expected him to move in tomorrow, but he made an excuse and put off the move until Monday—*after* Venus left.

Since he'd only known her a few days, he couldn't quite understand the flash of dread he felt at the thought of her leaving. Still, it was undeniable. He might not have known her long, but he knew he wanted every minute he could get with her. So he'd have to stay at Max's through the weekend. Max wouldn't mind. He'd been trying to talk Troy into staying on anyway. After last night, he didn't think Venus would mind, either.

Hit with a crisis involving a flooded mailing center at their north Georgia warehouse, Troy got so wrapped up with work that he forgot about calling Venus that morning. He thought about it while heading out for a lunch meeting, but since he was with the sales rep of one of their big textile providers, he decided to wait until he got back. They'd just sat down at their table in a nice restaurant in the Atlanta underground when he heard the trill of his cell phone, which he'd been about to turn off. He apologized and hit the answer button.

"Troy Langtree."

"You got a big package," Venus said.

He couldn't prevent a truly amused chuckle from escaping his mouth. His lunch companion eyed him curiously, and he turned slightly for privacy. "Thank you. Glad you approve."

She snorted. "Ha. I meant in the mail."

"Sure you did. Come on, you set that one up on purpose." He practically dared her to deny it.

"Okay," she admitted. "I did. And you went right for it, you dirty-minded thing."

"Just call me Mr. Black Kettle, Miss Pot."

She feigned offense. "Are you calling me dirty minded?"

"I would never do such a thing," he replied, knowing he sounded every bit as insincere as she had.

"While we're on the subject..."

"Yes?" he prodded.

She paused, then lowered her voice to a sultry, very satisfied-sounding whisper. "Wow."

He turned farther, almost covering the mouthpiece of the phone with his cupped hand. "Wow? Is that a good wow?"

"A most excellent wow." She sighed so deliberately it was almost a purr. He could suddenly picture her stretching out, extending her long, slim arms over her head, making her beautiful breasts rise up for his mouth, as she had last night.

He cleared his throat. "Wow works."

Seeing the sales rep glance at her watch, he murmured, "I should go. As for my...ahem...package, don't open it."

She sighed audibly. "It's from your department store."

"I know."

"It says it's from the Ladies' Department," she hinted.

He held back a chuckle. "I know."

Silence. She was probably trying to think of a way to get him to let her open it. Finally, she went for bluntness. "How will I know if I want to wear it if I don't get a chance to see it?"

"You're wearing it." His tone allowed for no argument.

Obviously not the tone to use with Venus. "Well, for your information, if it's a boring, typical little black cocktail dress, I'm so *not* wearing it."

Before he could reply, the sales rep leaned over and asked him if he knew where the ladies' room was. When he pointed, she got up, leaving him alone at the table. He knew Venus had to have heard the woman's voice. And of course karma was never kind enough to provide a bad cell phone connection when he needed one. Sure, it'd die out during an important business call, or if he broke down in the middle of the night somewhere. But certainly not right now when he had a woman on the line prepared to leap to the wrong conclusion.

"Where are you?" Her voice no longer sounded playful.

"At a lunch meeting. With a sales rep."

"A sales rep. A female one. Is she sixty and wrinkly?"

"No," he said, almost enjoying the flash of jealousy. "Probably thirty. Petite."

"Oh, thanks so much for sharing," she snapped.

"You asked."

"Which I shouldn't have. It was none of my business. I

was just curious about whether last night released you from your spell, and you've gone back to your full dogginess."

He didn't know whether to be amused or offended. Knowing Venus could be a lot more easily hurt than even she would admit, he replied with honesty. "Venus, she's happily married with kids, and she's a nice lady. This is a business lunch."

"Okay," she murmured, not sounding completely convinced.

"I'm damn sure not a saint..."

"No question," she muttered.

"You wouldn't want me so much if I were." He dared her to deny it—she stayed quiet. "I can honestly tell you, however, that I'm not interested in anyone except you."

She harrumphed into the phone, obviously not believing him. "It's not like it's any of my business, anyway. We had sex. We're not lovers or anything."

That really made him laugh. "Oh, honey," he said between chuckles, "we are *definitely* lovers. We've been lovers since the moment I touched your foot on the balcony Monday afternoon."

He heard her slow breaths as she absorbed his words, took them in, accepted them. They were, after all, nothing but the truth.

Then, finally, she whispered, "I won't open the package."

But he knew she would.

VENUS SWEATED for about nineteen and a half minutes after her conversation with Troy, then she finally tore the brown wrapping off the damn package. "He knows I will. He expects me to," she told herself. The realization should have made her more determined not to open it. Uh-uh. She just couldn't resist.

When she opened the box and found a plastic-wrapped bundle of emerald-green silk, she cooed. She pulled the dress out, breathless as she admired what Troy had selected for her.

She should have known the man would never go for something as simple as a little black cocktail dress. This was a glittery silk sheath. Slick and straight, it would fit like skin. Shot with gold threads, the fabric caught the light and sparkled like a jewel. It wasn't low cut, in fact it would fit tightly up around her neck. Judging by the high slit, however, what it didn't show in cleavage, it would make up for in leg.

The box contained everything else she'd need for tonight. Strappy, high-heeled sandals, along with a green silk bra and underwear so soft and silky they would feel like liquid against her skin. The man had very good taste.

Though she was dying to try everything on, she decided to shower first. It was already after one, and Max said they'd need to leave for the club by six. So, really, she'd done Troy a favor. Imagine she had waited for him to get home from work, and the dress hadn't fit? It wasn't as if she could have just pulled something out of her suitcase. *Hmm, the red spandex catsuit or the leopard-print halter and black leather miniskirt?*

That would have made for an interesting evening.

Besides, when Troy saw her in the dress, he'd forget he'd asked her not to open it. She hoped.

After showering, she dried her hair and took her time doing her nails. As she reached for the dress to try it on, someone knocked on her door. When she opened it, she saw the housekeeper, Mrs. Harris. The older woman smiled. "I wanted to see if you needed anything for tonight."

Surprised and touched by the offer, Venus shrugged. "Well, I don't think so. I have the dress." She nodded toward the closet door, where the dress was hanging.

"Beautiful," Mrs. Harris said with an approving nod. "Absolutely the perfect color on you."

"I do love emerald," she admitted, wondering how Troy had known her exact favorite shade of green.

"Of course, with your eyes, you would," the housekeeper replied. "Just like Miss Violet."

Venus raised a confused brow. "Who?"

"Mrs. Longotti."

"Her first name...was Violet?"

"Yes, didn't you know?"

No, she hadn't known. Max had never said anything. Then again, he'd been going out of his way to avoid talking about his son, or their possible relationship. So, of course, he hadn't talked about his wife either. "She died a long time ago?"

The woman nodded. "Yes, very long ago."

Venus sat on the edge of her bed. "She had green eyes?"

Mrs. Harris's expression conveyed her fondness for the woman. "Exactly the same shade as yours. And Max Jr.'s."

Max Jr. The reason she was here.

Somehow, in the excitement of getting to know Max, and, of course, of becoming involved with Troy, she'd nearly forgotten why she'd come to Atlanta. Since Leo hadn't been around for the past couple of days to remind her, she'd almost been able to convince herself this was simply a vacation. She hadn't sat down to think about what she was doing here—to determine if Max Longotti really could be her grandfather.

Somehow, though, as she considered the idea right now, in this home where she'd been so warmly welcomed and where she'd met two men who had become special to her, she couldn't say she minded the idea as much. That didn't mean she completely believed it. For the first time, however, she was willing to concede it might not be so awful. Yes, finding out it was true would mean giving up on her dream of someday finding her real father. But it would also mean that Max really was her family.

She honestly couldn't say she preferred to hold on to a phantom father when it was possible she might have a very alive, very real, very lovable grandfather. Venus swallowed hard. "Thank you for offering, Mrs. Harris, but I think I'm covered."

The woman began to walk out of the room, but paused to glance over her shoulder. "Would you like me to do your hair for you, Ms. Messina? I used to do Miss Violet's, and I believe I can still remember a few tricks."

Venus couldn't remember the last time anyone had done her hair for her. Other than color jobs or cuts, it had been ages since she'd sat still while someone brushed and curled and put her hair up. She nibbled her lip. "To be honest, I'm pathetic when it comes to anything except a basic braid or big, puffy curls. I'd love to put it up and do something fancy with it."

The broad smile on the other woman's face told Venus she hadn't been offering just to be polite. She really wanted to do this. She stared at Venus's head, lifting a long strand of hair, and nodding her head. "Yes, up in the back, with long tendrils beside your face. Perfect with the neckline of that dress."

"I should warn you, use a ton of spray on it," she said as Mrs. Harris led her to the vanity table. "This southern humidity has been killing me and it'll probably all be flat in no time."

"Oh, you'll get used to it," Mrs. Harris replied as she began going through Venus's hair supplies. "The best thing to do for the heat is to go for a late-night dip in the pool."

Venus felt a blush rising in her cheeks, but saw no secret meaning in the other woman's expression. "I'll have to do that."

If all her swims were as fabulous as the one the night before, she had a feeling she'd be doing a lot of swimming.

Over the next couple of hours, they joked and gossiped. As carefully as she could, Venus tried to draw the woman out about Max's family. His wife. His son. The kind of life they'd shared. The kind of man Max Jr. had been.

Apparently, quite a wonderful one.

Hearing stories about Max Jr.'s childhood—the way he could set anyone at ease, make even the most reserved person laugh—she very much wished she'd had a chance to get to know him.

Venus found herself enjoying the housekeeper's company. Mrs. Harris might have claimed not to have much experience with hair, but she knew a lot more than Venus did. She managed to create the kind of style Venus had never even attempted before—namely, simple, elegant and classy.

"Perfect," the woman said when Venus emerged from the bathroom, dressed, made-up, curled and primped to within an inch of her life.

Venus turned to look at herself in the full-length mirror, and froze. She knew the face, knew the features, but felt like she was staring at a stranger. She'd started the day as a bartender, and ended it as a red-haired Grace Kelly. "Well, Fairy Godmother, I think you should call me Cinderella. Wow."

The hairdo was a mass of swirls and curls, all tucked in at the back of her neck, with the exception of two long tendrils hanging over her shoulders. Her makeup was more subdued than she usually wore, but made her face look smoother, her lips fuller and her features more refined. The dress was a dream, as she'd known it would be, and it emphasized the green of her eyes.

"Wow, is right," a man's voice said. Glancing toward the door, Venus saw Troy standing there, watching from the hallway.

Surprised, she sucked in a breath. She hadn't even known he was home yet. Judging by his damp hair and smoothly shaved skin, as well as the crisp, navy suit he wore, he'd been back and getting ready for a while.

He looked amazing. As a woman who'd usually avoided guys in ties and instead dated men in hard hats or leather jackets, Venus didn't know that she'd ever fully appreciated how utterly perfect a man could look in a suit until she'd met Troy. He was a wicked Cary Grant, a modern Rhett Butler. A man who would look completely at home in a roomful of businessmen, but would secretly make every woman there want to slowly pull off that tie and undo the buttons of his white dress shirt with her teeth.

She was no exception.

Wondering if he was angry she'd opened the package, she gestured at the dress. "Thank you."

"You're welcome," he said as he strolled into the room. He walked around her, surveying her appearance from head to toe. Then he looked into her eyes. "You look absolutely beautiful, Venus. I figured that color would be great on you."

"You're not mad at me for opening it?"

"I knew you would."

She grinned. "I knew you knew I would."

Their smiles faded as they stared at one another. This was the first time they'd been face-to-face since Troy had left her bed this morning. Venus understood why he'd gone, but had missed him when she'd awakened. She'd almost needed that awkward morning after to try to get a hint as to where they were going from here. Were they, as he claimed, really lovers? Or would they revert to the tentative friendship they'd begun to form before last night?

"I think I'll go let Mr. Longotti know you two are ready," Mrs. Harris replied. Before she left, she took Venus's hand and gave it a squeeze. "Have a wonderful time tonight."

Venus thanked her yet again, then waited as the woman walked out, leaving her alone with Troy.

"Did Mrs. Harris help you with the makeup too?"

"Yes. Is it okay?" She cast a nervous glance at the mirror.

"Think you can put the lipstick back on by yourself?"

Knowing what he meant, she nodded and tilted her head back for his kiss. His lips touched hers gently, with tenderness she hadn't expected and wasn't quite prepared for. He cupped her cheek, then caressed her neck, all while tasting her lips like he'd never kissed her before.

Slipping her arms around his neck, she pressed against him, remembering the way his naked body had felt against hers. He obviously remembered too, and responded by deepening the kiss. Venus nearly whimpered as their tongues met and danced in a lazy, intimate kiss that sent warmth shooting through her body. When they finally parted, she stared into his eyes and whispered, "Thank you again. Can I confess I'm really glad you're going to be there with me tonight?"

Keeping his arms wrapped around her waist, he raised a brow. "You're not nervous, are you?"

She shrugged. "Shouldn't I be? I can't dance very well, and obviously my food preferences are a little limited."

"Just don't spit anything into your napkin," he said with a teasing laugh. "Besides, you don't have to try anything you don't think you'll like. Plenty of women who go to these things are too worried about their dress or their figures to eat much, anyway."

Venus cast a horrified glance down at her body encased in the outfit. "Okay, that cinches it—I'm not eating a bite."

"Babe, you have absolutely nothing to worry about." He gave her a look that could only be called a leer. "Your figure is perfect. After last night, I should know better than anyone."

"You knew that better than anyone on Monday. Remember your bathroom? Speaking of which, I haven't yet had a bath in that sunken tub of yours."

"Maybe tonight? I can wash your back." His eyes made it a promise, rather than an invitation. "Or would you rather meet me for another late-night swim?"

"Let's not limit ourselves. Both sound good." She pressed another quick kiss on his lips. "Now, I'd better fix my face."

Troy stayed and watched, leaning casually against the wall, his arms crossed in front of his chest as Venus reapplied her kissed-off lipstick. The scene felt surprisingly domestic, and it flustered her. She had to force her attention off his reflection in order to focus on applying her makeup.

"Okay," she said, squaring her shoulders and taking a deep breath. "The imposter is as ready as she'll ever be."

He tensed slightly. "Imposter?"

Suspecting he thought she'd been talking about her supposed relationship with Max, she clarified. "You know, the mouthy bartender dolled up as an elegant, sophisticated lady?"

"You're not an imposter."

"Yeah, I am. I'll be a fish out of water tonight, in spite of the fact that I look all...nice. Classy." She frowned. "Good."

Stepping closer, until their bodies were just inches apart, he kissed her temple. "Aww, don't worry honey. You're not good. You're just dressed that way."

She laughed at his reference to her Jessica Rabbit T-shirt.

"So, which is it?" he murmured as he kissed her again, this time on her cheek, close to her hairline. His whisper sent shivers of anticipation through her body as his warm breath touched her skin. "Are you not good? Or are you not bad?"

Swallowing as her senses filled with his closeness, with the amazingly tender way he kissed her face, as if she were the most perfect woman he'd ever seen, she said, "Maybe I'm both?"

He nodded. "Maybe that's why I like you so much."

He moved his lips to hers and kissed her lazily, ruining her lipstick again. Not that she cared. When he kissed her like that, so thoroughly and erotically, he was showing her the things he wanted to do with his mouth on other parts of her body.

Finally, she regained her senses and pulled away. "I'm

sure Max is waiting, and now I'm going to have to fix my makeup again. You might want to, uh, do some repair work yourself," she said. Grabbing a tissue, she wiped the traces of mauve off his well-kissed mouth. He nibbled lightly on her fingertip before she could draw her hand away.

"Behave," she scolded. "We've got to leave in a few minutes, and the last thing I need is for you to get me all hot and bothered before we go downstairs to meet Max."

She should have known better than to offer him such an irresistible temptation to be bad. He took her hand and brought it back up to his lips, kissing her knuckles, then her palm. "As I recall, you owe me some serious foreplay."

"Stop." Even to her own ears her voice sounded completely soft and unconvincing.

"We never did do everything I wanted to do last night."

Remembering some of the things *she'd* wanted to do, Venus wobbled on her high heels. To get him to stop seducing her with his words, not to mention his mouth, she tried to make a joke. "If I'd done some of the things I wanted to, I would probably have drowned."

"We were only in the pool the first time," he whispered as he pulled her hand up to encircle his neck, and leaned close to taste the skin just below her left ear.

"The first time. We...uh..."

He moved his hand to the small of her back, lightly stroking his fingers just above her backside. "Were frantic?"

"Uh-huh," she managed to whisper.

His leg slipped between hers, given easy access by the slit that bared her thigh almost to the very top. "Insatiable?"

"That too."

Before she realized what he was doing, he'd flattened his palm and run it down her body, pausing ever so briefly on her breast, before moving down to her stomach. Lower.

She shuddered.

"I needed to be inside you so much that first time, I didn't get a chance to explore you. To taste you like I wanted to."

Closing her eyes, she dropped her head back, picturing what he'd said. Moisture gathered between her legs. She leaned into him for support. "What about the other time?" she managed to ask.

"Wonderful," he said before kissing the corner of her mouth and nibbling on her lip. "But quieter. Sweeter."

Yes, it had been. Heartbreakingly tender, slow and delicious. "So," she murmured as he kissed her jaw, "we've done fast and frantic. And sweet and tender. What next?"

He lifted his head to stare down at her, and his answering smile was wickedly anticipatory. "Intoxicating and erotic."

A myriad of possibilities flooded her brain at that sultry promise. Troy was a sensory man, a deliberate man. A patient and confident man. He'd give his full attention to anything he attempted, in business...or in bed. The spark of heat in his eyes told her last night had merely been the beginning of something intense and mind-blowing. Another burst of lethargic desire spread through her body, warming her belly, loosening her limbs until she felt sure she couldn't remain standing.

Before she could respond, however, she heard a sound outside the bedroom door. Troy obviously did, too. He smoothly stepped back, just as they heard a knock. Max popped his head in and saw them together. "Almost ready?"

"Absolutely. Please, come in." Venus busied herself by reaching for the purse that had come with the dress.

"You're going to be the most beautiful woman there tonight, Venus. Troy, you're a lucky rascal."

Venus glanced back and forth between the men. "Troy?"

Max shrugged. "I'm afraid I'll have other responsibilities and won't be able to stay by your side all evening. One of which is to arrive an hour early, so I'm on my way now. The car is downstairs. Troy, can you bring Venus and find your way?"

Troy nodded. "Of course."

"And I don't want Venus having to fend off all those no-good, lazy playboys at the club. So you'll stay by her side?"

Straightening his tie, Troy gave Venus an intimate look. "I can promise I won't let her out of my sight for a minute until she's back here in this bed, safe and sound."

And he'd be right here with her. *Intoxicating and erotic.*

She wondered if Max could sense the current of excitement snapping between them. Not that she worried Max would disapprove of their involvement. In fact, when she thought about it, she had a feeling he wouldn't mind a bit. In spite of his wealth, Max was a very down-to-earth person, with a sharp wit and a true appreciation for other sharp-minded people. The way he often spoke about Troy had made her realize he liked him very much.

Still, she didn't want the old gentleman to think badly of her. Her concern had absolutely nothing to do with Leo Gallagher's demand that she be discreet. Instead, she simply found herself caring about Max's opinion.

Maybe she was too reckless on occasion. Or, at least,

had been when she was younger and hungry to be loved. Maybe so wanting to have a family of her own, to belong to someone, had made her sell herself short when it came to relationships.

But what was happening between her and Troy was different. Because, whether he realized it or not, whether they admitted it aloud or not, in some ways they were two of a kind. They spoke the same language, even though they used completely different words. They had the same drives, though they were on different paths. They'd fallen into a perfect harmony the moment they'd met, though they argued whenever they were together.

They were, she believed, very well matched. Whether that equaled a relationship for a week, or a lifetime, she couldn't say. Nor, right this minute, did she much care. For tonight, at least, she was going to be Cinderella enjoying the ball. And enjoying what happened when she got back home even more.

How appropriate for a Jersey princess with a checkered past to hook up with a prince charming who was a self-confessed dog.

"Mrs. Harris told me what color dress you were wearing tonight," Max said. He cleared his throat and tugged at his tie. "I have had these things lying around for years, with no one to wear them. You might get some use out of them." He reached into his suit pocket and pulled out a velvet box, handing it to her. "It's up to you. If they're too old-fashioned…"

Seeing what lay inside the box, Venus immediately shook her head and took a step back. She raised her hand, palm out. "I can't. That stuff probably costs more than I make in a year."

No way could she wear the dangly emerald earrings and stunning emerald-and-diamond bracelet. Fancy dress and hairdo or not, she was not cut out to wear jewels fit for a princess.

"I'm a walking catastrophe when it comes to jewelry," she said with a forced laugh. "If I dropped an earring down the sink or lost the bracelet in a punch bowl, I'd never forgive myself."

"I doubt you're going to be seeing any punch bowls at the club," Troy murmured with a wry chuckle.

"I was speaking figuratively," she snapped.

A knowing, completely understanding smile widened Max's lips, and his blue eyes held such an expression of tenderness, she nearly cried. "Refuse them if you don't like them, Venus. But, please, don't refuse them because you think you're not worthy." Placing the box on the table beside the bed, he took her hand and snapped the bracelet onto it.

Seeing that he would not be dissuaded, Venus put one, then the other, of the beautiful dangly earrings on her ears. "Thank you, Max. I promise you I'll take good care of them. And I'll return them the minute we get home."

Max nodded. "I know you will. Just avoid the punch bowl."

She rolled her eyes at the joke.

"Now, would you mind if Troy or Mrs. Harris took a picture of us together?" the old man asked, sounding slightly unsure of how she'd react. "I'd like to have one...but only if you agree."

Venus stared at the man, usually so confident and strong. "Of course I don't mind." At his look of visible relief, Venus drew in a deep breath. This obviously meant a great deal to Max.

"Thank you again for the use of the jewelry," she said as he gallantly offered his arm to lead her out of the room.

"They're as perfect on you as I knew they'd be. Your eyes, just the same..."

Though almost afraid to, she wanted to be sure of what he'd been about to say. "As?"

"As hers," he replied, his voice soft and reminiscent. A gentle smile softened his craggy features. "As my Violet's."

Venus didn't say another word as they proceeded downstairs.

9

THE COUNTRY CLUB wasn't all *that*.

It was okay, Venus decided when they arrived, But no fancier than any four-star hotel in Baltimore. The white columned entrance didn't seem quite as grand as Max's house. The chandeliers were normal size, not tremendously ornate. The furniture was standard banquet issue—round tables for eight, padded metal-framed chairs. The food she worked up the nerve to try was pretty good, but the drinks were definitely a little too heavy on the mixer and the ice.

The people, however, were just about what she'd expected. Max introduced both her and Troy as friends from out of town, nothing more. He didn't clarify that they were friends from *different* towns, and some people seemed to assume they were a couple. A misconception Troy didn't go out of his way to correct, she quickly realized. She liked that he didn't.

They were dressed tastefully and spoke serenely, but Venus couldn't miss the speculation in the eyes of some of those she met. The wealthy women judged her dress, noted the emeralds and greeted her warmly. The unattached men judged her figure *under* the dress, noted the absence of a ring, and tried to pick her up. On the few occasions when she found herself alone she came across the typical smooth-talking, flirtatious guys and their sharp-eyed, possessive dates. Seemed like things were pretty much the same with the rich set as they were with the Flanagan's crowd.

"Having a nice time?" Troy asked as he returned from the bar, carrying a glass of wine for her. She was standing near the patio doors, watching the dancers in the center of the tastefully decorated banquet room.

"It's okay."

"So far no one's called you an imposter, have they?"

"The night is still young."

An anticipatory smile was his only answer. She suddenly knew what he was thinking. Yes, the night was still young, and he'd made some rather suggestive promises about how it would end. *Intoxicating. Erotic.* She shivered in anticipation.

"Are you chilly?"

"No, fine," she replied.

"Good, let's dance."

She shook her head. "Sorry, dancing's not one of my strong suits. I'm about as graceful as a clown on roller skates."

He took her drink from her hand and set it down on a table, along with his own. "Just follow me."

She remained rooted where she stood. Hiding her absolute terror of going out onto the dance floor in front of all these people, she tried to go on the attack. "In case you haven't figured it out yet, I don't follow any man."

Taking her arm, he leaned closer. "I know that about you already. Just follow my lead on the dance floor. It's a legal excuse for me to have you in my arms in front of these people."

Well, when he put it that way...

Venus caught Max's eye as she and Troy walked on to the dance floor. He gave her a small nod, still chatting with the club set, who'd given him an award earlier in the evening for some of his charitable work. Another reason to admire the man—apparently, from the glowing remarks of the head of some committee or another, Max had spent a fortune helping to finance a summer youth camp program for underprivileged kids.

"Venus?" Troy asked, waiting patiently for her to step into his arms. She did so, immediately slipping her arms around his neck. He paused, then gently pulled one hand into his, and laced his fingers with hers. The other he placed on his shoulder.

"Look, my dance experience is the type where the girl wraps her arms around the guy's neck and he plants his on her butt," she said with a sigh. "Then they rub against each other to the music while they make out and wait for the lights to come up."

He chuckled, easing her closer until their bodies nearly touched from neck to knee. "I wouldn't mind that kind of dancing. But try it my way this time, okay?" Troy said. Then he began to move, indicating by the brush of his thigh against hers, or a slight squeeze of his hand, which way he was going.

Venus almost surprised herself at how quickly she was able to catch on. The song was strictly Muzak, but she found herself almost liking it, feeling the rhythm as she began to relax in Troy's arms. Catching sight of the two of them in the reflection of a mirror over the bar, she hid a smile, thinking she did feel very much like Cinderella.

Troy probably wouldn't appreciate the comparison to Prince Charming, who, even she had to admit, had been something of a wimp. Troy wasn't the kind of man who'd rely on a glass slipper instead of his own eyes to track down the girl at the end of the story. Actually, when she thought about it, Troy probably would have seduced the poor thing into his palace bachelor pad, making her miss her midnight curfew altogether.

She probably wouldn't have given a damn.

"You must do this a lot," she said. "You're good."

"Believe it or not, my mother forced us to take lessons when Trent and I were kids."

She should have known he'd dance as well as he did everything else. As they moved to the music, she began to count the number of women who eyed him approvingly or, in some cases, hungrily. She lost count when she ran out of fingers. And toes.

"You're doing very well, too," he said. "Though, sometime, I'd like to try your kind of dancing. You've definitely put an image into my mind." He lowered his voice. "Particularly since I know better than anyone what you have on under your clothes."

Knowing he was referring to the underwear accompanying the dress, Venus bit her lip and lowered her eyes. "Uh, sorry to break it to you, but I'm not wearing them."

He missed a step. "You have nothing on under that dress?"

She practically snorted. "Puh-lease. I haven't gone braless since a month after I hit puberty."

He sighed.

"But," she admitted, "I'm not wearing the panties."

Troy honestly tried to focus on the dance. Particularly since they were in the middle of a floor crowded with other couples, some less than graceful and prone to bumping into anyone in a ten-foot radius. But at Venus's saucy announcement, he missed another step. "You're really bad."

"I thought we'd already established that," she said, tossing her head and raising a brow.

"And I thought you were kidding when you said you don't wear underwear."

"Oh, you remember that, do you?"

Remember it? Remember her lying on the floor beside her bed, her sweet, naked butt the first sight he'd seen when he walked into her bedroom the other morning?

Yeah. He definitely remembered.

"I was kidding," she finally admitted, her green eyes still sparkling with merriment.

"When were you kidding? Tuesday morning?" He glanced down at her dress, looking for any seams. He saw none. "Or now?"

Though it was probably wicked, he couldn't help hoping she didn't mean now. The idea of having her in his arms, in public, wearing a dress that felt like silky skin beneath his hands, bare from the waist down beneath it, was incredibly erotic.

"Tuesday," she admitted, her smile sultry. She obviously knew what he'd been thinking. "I do wear them most of the time."

"And tonight?"

She shrugged, drawing out the expectation with her silence. Then, finally, she shook her head.

He moved one hand down her back, continuing the dance. Resting his palm below her waist, just above the curve of her backside, he pulled her closer, letting her feel the way he'd reacted to the provocative image her confession had inspired.

Her eyes widened and he thought he heard a sound almost like a whimper. "I think I like your kind of dancing, too," she admitted, pressing her body even closer.

"Good. Because I can't walk off this floor right now," he growled into her ear. "Are you going to tell me why you're not wearing...anything?"

"They were very pretty, but I don't do thongs."

"Oh?"

She shook her head. "A friend of mine swears by them and got me to try them once. Frankly, I just don't like feeling as if my cheeks are being flossed all night."

He couldn't prevent laughter from spilling out of his mouth. A few people on the dance floor looked over, but he ignored them.

"I suppose you had nothing else you could have worn?"

"Nope," she said, completely unapologetic. "A dress this fabulous required something more special than anything I had in my suitcase."

He nodded. "I agree with your reasoning. Much more special this way. There's only one problem, the way I see it."

She raised an inquisitive brow.

"That dress is silk. It tends to show moisture." He brushed his lips across the tendril of hair at her temple, letting her feel his breaths. Moving his hand lower, until his fingers caressed the curve of her rear, he continued. "So you'd better be very careful not to get it wet."

Her body tensed. This time, it was Venus who missed a step. He moved his hand around to her hip. "Or is it too late?"

"It was probably too late before we left the house," she admitted, her voice thick and husky.

He swallowed, imagining her wet and ready for him. He remembered how slick and sweet she'd been the night before, the way she'd cried out when he'd caressed that hot flesh between her legs. Right now, he wanted to be inside her again more than he wanted to keep breathing. "Let's get the hell out of here."

"What about Max?"

"We have two cars."

She smiled slightly. "Lucky thing."

"If Max hadn't found a reason for riding separately, I would have."

"Oh? How?"

"I have no idea," he admitted. "But I would have come up with something."

Pressing against his body, she could feel the hard-on straining against his suit trousers. "I think you've already come up with something."

"Yeah," he growled. "It's going to stay that way, and we're going to have to keep dancing, if you don't knock it off."

No way were they sticking around any longer than necessary. She stepped back so quickly she nearly bumped into someone dancing behind them.

He grinned. "Anxious?"

"Dying."

"Ditto."

Luckily, Venus managed to behave herself for the next dance, until Troy felt in control enough to walk off the floor. They stopped to tell Max they were heading out, and he didn't seem to mind at all. In fact, he went out of his way to tell them to enjoy themselves at the house, since he would have to stay here for another couple of hours. This wasn't the first time Max had looked at him and Venus with a hint of understanding in his eyes. Troy liked knowing he had the elderly man's silent blessing.

They waited quietly while the valet brought his car around to the front entrance of the club. Troy didn't so much as hold her arm, not trusting himself to put one finger on her because his need for her was so great. She appeared to be having a similar problem. She held her body straight and rigid, not meeting his eye, not until after they were in the car, pulling down the long driveway.

Troy made it about fifty yards away from the entrance before pulling off the side of the road. He stopped the car and reached for Venus. "I can't wait."

She unfastened her seat belt, leaning closer as their mouths met in a hot, frenzied kiss. "Me, neither."

"God, I want you so much," he muttered, tugging her closer. He lifted her right off her seat, placing her sideways in his lap. She wriggled her bottom against him, whimpering as she felt the raging erection that had returned.

They kissed again and again, their tongues hungrily mating as the heat in the car went from simmering to explosive.

"I told you this car is too damn small," she muttered with a wince when they parted for air.

Glancing down, he saw the gear shift digging into her hip. "Here." He slipped his hand down her body, until he reached her thigh. While he shifted her so her back was pressed against his chest, he tugged her dress up and her legs apart, then placed one of her sandal-clad feet on the seat she'd just vacated. The other was on the floor, right next to his own.

The high slit in the front of the dress fell open, revealing those beautiful toned legs, invitingly splayed open, the gear shift between her parted knees.

"Better?"

"Oh, much," she said with a sigh as she turned her face to stare at him, her eyes hungry.

He agreed. The position was perfect. Her warm bottom fit snugly on his lap. She lifted her arm behind her head and turned her head up, tugging him down for another one of those wet, frenzied kisses. His own hands were free to explore her.

She nearly purred as he slid his palm higher up her thigh. "Checking to see if I was lying?"

"I know you weren't lying, Venus," he said. "I'm just accepting the invitation you issued when you left your underwear at home."

She silently invited him again, parting her legs wider, urging him on. When he finally reached the apex of her thighs, he found her warm, wet, and open. And, of course, unclothed.

Slipping his fingers between her slick folds, he heard her breath catch in her throat. He kissed her again, absorbing her whimpers and moans with his mouth as he slid one finger deep inside her and toyed with her clitoris with his thumb.

"You're going to make me come right on the side of the road, where someone could drive past at any second," she said, sounding both indignant and excited as hell.

"Yeah," he replied, completely unapologetic. "I am."

She smiled, then kissed him again, rocking her body against his fingers. The heady smell of sex filled the quiet car, the silence interrupted only by the sounds of their harsh breathing and her helpless whimpers. She was beautiful, open and responsive beneath his hands. Completely trusting. Intoxicatingly feminine.

Entirely his.

When her frenzy intensified, he took her higher until she shuddered and moaned her completion. She shook beneath his hand, her muscles contracting as her body was overcome with her rush of pleasure.

Troy watched her, saw the flush rise in her face, and her lips part as she gasped for air. Her eyes were nearly closed, her head tilted back. She bit her lip as she shook with her powerful climax. Venus was an incredibly responsive woman, and it took all his willpower to avoid following her over the edge.

He moved his hand to lightly caress her thigh and hip. Then, kissing her jaw, he whispered, "You're incredible."

Her breathing hadn't even yet returned to normal when she turned around and reached for his zipper. "So are you."

"I think in this instance you're right—the car's too small," he said with a heartfelt sigh, wishing right now that he'd bought a damn station wagon. Or a minivan. Or a bus.

She shook her head, undeterred, and eased the zipper down. Scooting off his lap, she knelt in the passenger seat and gave him a wicked look. "Fair's fair."

When she freed him from his trousers and cupped him in her hand, he jerked up, unable to resist the touch of her cool fingers against his heated skin. "Venus..."

"Shh," she said as she reached across him, her upper body in his lap, her curvy rear sticking up in the next seat. He paused to appreciate the view until she pushed the seat release lever. Troy fell back in the car to a reclining position. He had to laugh at her determination. Then she moved over him, again sitting on his lap, but this time face-to-face.

"Hot, fast sex in the car. This isn't exactly as intoxicating and erotic as I'd planned," he told her.

"This is erotic as hell," she replied with certainty. "Besides, considering we've been having verbal foreplay for hours, I have a feeling this is just going to be an appetizer. You need to blow off steam to get ready for the main course."

He groaned, picturing all the things he planned to do

to her when they got home. Main course was a pretty apt description, as he planned to feast on every inch of her long, luscious body.

Venus slid down, closer now, holding her wet opening just out of reach of his straining erection. Unable to resist, he thrust up, entering her the tiniest bit. Her eyes widened. "Impatient, are you?"

He responded by encircling her head with his hands, his fingers twisting into her hair as he pulled her down for a slow, wet kiss. "You're not?" he whispered against her lips. Their kiss was carnal, filled with promise, heat and desire. He moved again, surging a little deeper.

But not nearly deep enough. "Have mercy," he whispered.

Before she could reply, a bright flash of light lit up the interior of the still-running car. Venus's eyes widened in panic as she rose to peek out the back windshield. "A car. Coming from the country club."

She was off his lap and in her seat so fast, he wondered if he'd imagined he'd been an inch inside her eight seconds before.

He groaned, then grabbed the seat lever and brought himself up to a sitting position. "I think we'd better go. Another near miss and I'm not going to give a damn if it's Max, or the president of the charitable society, or the state police."

They sat silently, watching a car drive by, its occupants staring out the windows in abject curiosity as they passed.

"I think you're right. Let's get home," she murmured, obviously still as aroused and ready as he.

He threw the Jaguar into gear and hit the gas, turning toward Max's estate. The thick silence in the car remained heady with expectation as they drove.

He'd never known a more erotic woman, and had never imagined the intoxication of being with someone so fully in tune with her desires. He just didn't know quite *how* anxious she was. At least, not until she reached into his lap again. "What are you..."

"Shh," she whispered. "You have to blow off that steam, or my night is just going to be ruined."

He only knew what she meant when she bent down over his lap and put her lips over him.

"Holy hell," he muttered, managing to keep the car on the road as she engulfed him with her warm, wet mouth. "You can't..."

"I can," she whispered as she pressed kisses all over his erection and reached into his pants to gently stroke him. "And I am. So get used to it and get us home."

Get used to it? Get used to heat and warmth and silky wetness sucking him deeper and deeper toward absolute bliss?

Okay, yeah, he could get used to it. He just didn't know if he could concentrate on driving long enough to stay alive to get used to it! "Venus, you have to stop," he said as she wrung a deep moan of pleasure from his throat. "I could crash."

"Think of how that'd look in the papers," she whispered, her breaths tickling his sensitive skin. She nibbled, licked again, then sucked him deeper. "New Atlanta executive crashes during oral pleasure with plucky Baltimore bartender."

His laugh segued into another long, guttural groan. He pressed the gas pedal harder, seeing the exit for Buckhead, dying to get home to end this incredibly erotic torture.

He'd just spotted the gates outside Max's driveway when he felt the signaling waves of anticipation roll through his body. He was close. Very close. "Holy mother..."

"Are we home yet?"

"You have to stop," he told her, his voice ragged and nearly out of control as he cruised the car up the driveway. He was hardly mindful of the trees lining the drive, maneuvering by instinct rather than sight.

"Oh, but I don't want to stop," she insisted as she lowered her mouth over him again.

He hit the brakes beneath the porte cochere, throwing the car into Park and grabbing her by the shoulders about ten seconds before too late. Hauling her up, he pulled her mouth to his and kissed her, absorbing her taste and her frenzy.

She tasted erotic. Of sex and intimacy. And endless, mindless pleasure. Their tongues tangled and met even as she moved her hand to his lap in order to coax him into that final, body-rocking climax.

When it was over, when he was drained and spent, he sagged back in his seat. Troy waited for an outside light to flip on, for the housekeeper or a maid to open the front door and catch them in the car in this incriminating position.

Frankly, my dear, I don't give a damn.

"I'm sorry, I think I ruined your pants," she whispered.

"Screw the pants."

She smiled lazily. "Okay, Troy, that was the appetizer. But don't think for a minute you're off the hook for the intoxicating and erotic."

"Deal," he muttered. "Now, give me five minutes to get my brain working again and we can go inside and get started."

Merciless, Venus grabbed for the door handle. "You've

got five seconds." She hopped out of the car, anxious to get up to her room, or Troy's, and get naked with him. Oral sex and orgasms were lovely. But she wanted more. A lot more.

Biting a cheek to hide her grin, she watched as Troy adjusted himself, then took his suit coat off and draped it over his arm. The coat did an effective job of covering the crotch of his pants. But she doubted anything could disguise the smell of passion they both exuded. Thankfully, they didn't run into Mrs. Harris or anyone else when they entered the dark, quiet house.

His was the first doorway off the top of the stairs, so that's where they stopped, by unspoken consent. Once inside, he shut and locked the door, then dropped the coat.

"Do you still need five minutes?" she asked. She reached for her zipper, knowing he didn't. She'd learned the night before that Troy wasn't one of those men who needed a lot of down time.

He shook his head and took her into his arms, pulling her hands down to her sides and holding them there. "Now we're on my clock, honey." He kissed her lightly, licking her lips in a quick tease, then pulling away to nibble on her cheek, her earlobe and her neck. "So it's time to slow down." His whisper sent warm breath against her flesh and tingles down her spine. He kissed her again, still teasing, still building this at his own pace. "The pool was yours, Venus," he whispered against her throat. Then he laughed softly, a wicked laugh full of anticipation and seduction. "So was the car..."

He almost dared her to dispute his final words. "But the rest of the night's all mine."

She grabbed the dresser to steady herself on legs that felt as limp as jelly. Her pulse roared in her ears and she moaned, certain of one thing: Troy was going to take his time and deliver everything his self-confidence had promised he could from the moment she'd first set eyes on him. Like a cocky baseball player pointing to the grandstand as he took the plate, he was promising her one hell of a home run.

"You're in control all night?" she managed to ask through harshly indrawn breaths.

He nodded, allowing for no argument. "All night."

His anticipatory expression told her he intended to use his time very wisely. He would not be rushed like their first time in the water. Nor would he be as slow, tender and sweet as he'd been the second time they'd made love on the chaise lounge.

Slow, yes. But sweet, oh, no. His eyes didn't promise sweetness. They promised wicked, sensual torture.

She shivered in anticipation. A Troy frenzied with desire and desperate to have her she could handle. Because that's how he made her feel. But a Troy deliberately seductive, painstakingly thorough and completely in control, would likely be the most intensely erotic experience of her life. She could either fight for a more equal footing by trying to seduce him until he was as mindless and needy as she. Or, she could give up, let him take over and do every delightful thing he could imagine to her.

Hmm, life's full of tough choices.

This sure as hell wasn't one of them.

"All right, Troy."

He nodded, as if he'd never had any doubt about her response. "Come here," he ordered, walking away toward the bed. He didn't turn to see if she'd follow, knowing, of course, that she couldn't resist. He undid his tie, pulling it off and throwing it to the floor, then he unbuttoned the top few buttons of his shirt.

Venus slowly approached, nibbling on her lip, nearly unable to breathe because of the excitement roaring through her veins. "Here?" she asked when she reached the king-size bed.

He nodded, then made a turning motion with his finger. She obeyed, turning around until her back was to him. His touch was deliberately light, barely brushing the sensitive spot on the back of her neck as he reached for the zipper of her dress and began tugging it down. The zipper opened slowly, the hiss of the separating teeth the only sound in the room.

As every inch of skin was revealed, he followed the path with his mouth. He kissed her lightly, nibbling on her spine, inhaling deeply as if savoring the scent of her body. He tasted every bit of her, memorizing her with his lips and tongue.

The zipper was a long one, ending well below her waist, almost between the curves of her rear. By the time he had it all the way down, Troy was kneeling on the floor behind her. Her breath caught in her throat as he continued to kiss her, and Venus forced herself to relax. To accept what he wanted to give her. To be patient enough to enjoy the delight of each step, rather than rushing to the climax, in spite of how much she ached to have him inside her.

"Have I told you yet I'm glad you didn't wear the underwear?" he asked as he moved his mouth lower, his warm breaths reaching the top curves of her bottom.

She moaned, dying to see him, to watch him, but forcing herself to stay still. "I think I figured that out in the car."

"Ahh, the car. That's one for you." He gently nipped at her hip. "And one for me. Let's check the score in the morning."

Score? He meant orgasms. Lots and lots of them.

She began to shake.

"Drop the dress," he murmured, continuing to press hot kisses across the small of her back.

With a lift of her shoulders, the fabric fell away, puddling at her feet. He lifted her foot, letting her step out of the dress, then tossing it aside. Circling her ankles, he slid his hands up her legs, touching them from foot to hip. "Mmm," he whispered, as if delighting in the texture of her skin, the way one would enjoy the sensory feel of soft velvet or satin.

She couldn't see him. But she felt each touch, each scrape of his finger on her body. Every exhalation he made against her flesh was another caress. Every dip of his tongue made her arch back toward him in invitation.

He continued to stroke her legs, moving down with such slow precision she ached, waiting to see where he'd touch her next. Finally, he gently eased her foot out of one shoe, then the other, taking time to caress even her toes. He seemed to take great delight in nibbling the back of her hip, and the curve of her bare backside. She hissed when he moved lower, kissing the vulnerable spot where her right cheek met the back of her thigh. Then he nudged one of her legs forward, pushing it up until her knee rested on the bed. A gentle push with his hand told her he wanted her to bend forward slightly, and she complied.

Venus realized what he intended one second before she felt his tongue slide over her hot, wet flesh.

"Oh, God," she moaned, dropping her head back and closing her eyes. He was below her, tasting her, drawing all the nerve endings in her body together in one wet, throbbing spot that he suckled and tasted with perfect precision and obvious delight. And when she shuddered and cried out with her orgasm, she thought she heard him whisper against her inner thigh, "That's two."

10

TROY TOOK PITY ON HER over the course of the night and stopped counting out loud at five. But, as he gradually awoke the next morning, knowing by the angle of the sun slanting into his bedroom that he'd overslept again, he had to figure Venus had hit at least seven or eight on the orgasm meter. He chuckled.

A most satisfying night.

Not just for her. Definitely not. Troy didn't think he'd ever had a more erotic experience in his life.

He couldn't get enough of her. He'd loved every kiss, every taste and worshipped every inch of her. The sound of her cries and moans had thrilled him as much as the look of heady delight on her face. Venus had been so trusting, so responsive, so open to everything, from gentle teasing to erotic massage. When he took her to the heights of pleasure, she'd playfully challenge him to take her higher—a challenge he couldn't resist.

Their entire night had been one enticing moment after another as they'd made love for hours. Troy had used all of his control to focus only on her. Touching her. Tasting her. Indulging in her while keeping himself in check. He'd managed to bring her to the point where she was sobbing in desperation before he finally took her. And that, too, had gone on forever because she'd so wisely helped him "blow off steam" in the car.

Troy thought of himself as someone who knew his way

around the bedroom. Lord knew, he'd had enough experience. But last night, in Venus's arms, when he'd realized how much he loved looking into her eyes, realized that he'd never felt anything as perfect as the smoothness of her skin, he knew it was about more. There had been desire, yes. But also, he had to admit, emotion.

"Crazy," he told himself as he got out of bed, eyeing the pile of blankets on the floor where they'd kicked them.

Crazy maybe. Still, it was true. He liked her more than he'd ever liked any woman. He wasn't crazy enough to call it love, because, after all, he'd only known her for a few days. Besides, Troy had never truly believed he'd ever fall in love.

So his feelings for Venus confused him. If not love... what?

He'd wanted her from the moment they'd met. More importantly, he'd liked her wit, liked her sharp, sassy comments. He'd admired her self-confidence and her attitude. He'd enjoyed her company, been challenged by her, always wondering but never quite sure just what she was thinking or what she'd do next.

Probably most telling of all, he absolutely dreaded the thought of her leaving on Sunday.

Then again, if she turned out to be Max's granddaughter, she could end up staying in Atlanta for a while. Though Max and Venus hadn't talked any more about DNA tests or birth certificates, Troy found himself wanting them to hurry things along. "So she'll stay," he whispered.

Damn. Maybe he really was falling in love with her.

He didn't spend a lot of time evaluating that thought. It was too early in the morning to wonder if his horndog days really were behind him and he would be able to settle down to one amazing, vibrant, sensual woman. "Venus."

Missing her, though she'd left his bed only a couple of hours before, he tugged on some shorts. He washed, then went to her room, noting the open door. Peeking inside and seeing her empty bed, he figured she'd already gone down to breakfast.

Instead of showering and getting dressed for work, as he should have, Troy headed downstairs, too, still wearing only a pair of shorts. Something Max had said during the party last night, about how much Venus loved roller coasters, had stuck with him. Judging by the look in Max's eye when he'd planted the idea in his head, he didn't think the older man would mind him taking a day off. Venus would probably really enjoy a trip to a local theme park just outside Atlanta.

That is, if she had the energy to walk today.

His own step was light as he descended the stairs, a whistle on his lips. Hearing voices in the dining room, he turned toward it. Then, however, a flash of red caught his eye through the French doors leading to the family room.

Only one thing on earth with that particular shade could make his heart speed up.

He pushed the door open, preparing to greet a sexy, thoroughly satisfied Venus. Instead, he froze just inside the door. She was here all right, dressed scantily in a sexy bikini.

And in the arms of another man.

In spite of her long, sleepless night Venus had awakened early, still too keyed up, physically and emotionally, to remain in bed. *What an amazing night.*

Troy had not only delivered what he'd silently promised since the moment they'd met, he'd hands-down blown her out of the ballpark. Grand slam couldn't begin to describe it. *Wow.*

It was during their 2:00 a.m. bath in his sunken tub, when she'd been reclining between his legs—her back against his chest, her head on his shoulder—that she realized she was going to have to leave him soon. Just a few more days and she'd be out of Troy's life, back to Baltimore, back to her own world.

Whatever happened with Max, Venus truly couldn't see herself staying here in his home. If she did turn out to be his grandchild, an idea that somehow didn't seem so horrifying anymore, she hoped they could develop a good relationship in spite of the physical distance between them. She just couldn't picture herself living here permanently. This was a fun vacation, playing Cinderella at the castle. But all vacations had to come to an end. She had to go back to her real world.

Besides, she missed her friends and her apartment—surly cat, dying ferns and all. She missed Uncle Joe and Flanagan's.

But she was honest enough to admit one thing—she suspected none of that would compare with how she'd feel leaving Troy on Sunday. It amazed her that someone she hadn't known a week ago could now seem to be the most important person in her world. She hadn't expected it, but somewhere along the way, she'd fallen head over heels in...*something* for Troy Langtree.

Real love? What Venus knew about real love she'd learned from her mother and foster mother. She knew next to nothing about romantic love, so she couldn't be one hundred percent sure.

But it felt pretty darn close.

She'd lain awake this morning, marveling at that fact, until she finally had to get up and go do something. Figuring Troy would still be sound asleep, she'd donned her bikini and gone out to the pool to swim some laps.

Afterward, feeling much more ready to face the day, she'd headed back inside to change for breakfast. She'd paused when she spied Troy standing inside the family room. He'd had his back to her, and she'd hidden a mischievous chuckle as she snuck up on him. She'd paused long enough to admire the view from the rear. She'd never seen Troy dressed in faded jeans and a tight black T-shirt like what he wore this morning. "Why don't you wear jeans more often?" She reached out and squeezed his taut butt. "You definitely do some *fine* things for them, darlin'."

He'd jerked, as if startled. Before he could say a word, she'd slipped her arms around him and pressed her mouth to his.

He sucked in a breath, probably shocked that she'd risk kissing him where someone could walk in at any time, but Venus couldn't help it. Since she'd quietly left his bed just a few hours before, she'd begun to acknowledge how she felt about the man. She'd fallen for him, big time, and wanted nothing more than to be in his arms to revel in her newfound feeling.

Unfortunately, she realized almost instantly something was wrong. Troy wasn't kissing her back.

She tried again, cupping his cheek, turning her head to the side as she tangled her fingers in his hair. Then something bright and shiny caught her eye. A small, gold hoop dangled from his pierced earlobe—an earlobe which had *not* been pierced when she'd been sucking on it just hours before.

"What the hell is that on your ear?" she asked, shocked enough to drop her arms and take a step back.

"That would be an earring," a woman's smooth voice replied. "My *husband's* earring."

Completely in shock, Venus turned toward the doorway. Standing there, looking utterly shocked, was another Troy.

He was still tousled from his bed, all warm and rumpled. Definitely the man whose chest she'd nibbled on enough to leave a visible love bite—which she could see even from here. Directly behind him stood a petite, obviously pregnant, brunette.

"Oh, crap," she muttered. Pressing a completely humiliated hand over her eyes, Venus took a step away from the guy in jeans—who had to be Troy's twin brother, Trent.

Trent started to laugh. So did the pregnant woman—his wife, obviously—who sidestepped Troy and walked across the room. She extended her hand. "Hi, I'm Chloe. You must be Venus."

All Venus could do was nod and shake the woman's hand. If the situations had been reversed, and she'd walked in on her husband in the arms of a half-naked woman trying to stick her tongue down his throat, Venus didn't think she would have been quite as friendly. Her hand wouldn't have been extended for a shake. More likely for a slap. Or a punch.

"I'm so sorry," she whispered, still feeling awful, in spite of the genuine smile on the pretty young woman's face. "I honestly thought…"

"That Trent was Troy," Chloe finished. "Don't sweat it. You're not the first, and you probably won't be the last. It took me a long time to tell them apart, too."

"That's an understatement," Trent murmured as he slid an arm across his wife's shoulders.

Venus finally worked up the nerve to look at Troy. He

didn't appear too happy and certainly wasn't handling the situation with the same good humor as his sister-in-law. In fact, his usually bright eyes were somewhat stormy.

"Troy, I'm really sorry. I feel like an idiot."

He slowly crossed the room, his mouth tight and his jaw set. Ignoring the other two, he focused only on Venus. Taking her chin in his hand, he lifted her face to his. "You can always tell us apart," he said, his tone controlled and confident. "I'm the one who tastes like *this.*"

Then, completely uncaring of the other couple, or the still-open door, he brought his mouth to hers in a hot, insistent kiss. His lips parted as he ravenously tasted her tongue with his own, igniting liquid flame in her body.

Moaning, Venus met every sweet stroke. She pressed against him, curling her fingers into the crisp hair on his chest. Forgetting everyone else in the world, she could only think about what this man had made her feel the night before. What he'd made her feel since the moment they'd met.

Her heart pounded in her chest and her knees grew weak. She almost collapsed against him, unable to focus on anything except how much she adored being exactly where she was—in Troy's arms.

"I think she gets the picture," someone said with dry amusement. The wife. Chloe? Was that her name? Heck, she could barely even remember her own right now!

Troy finally began to pull away, pressing one or two more sweet kisses against the corner of her mouth before stepping back. He kept his arm around her waist and turned to face his brother and sister-in-law. Venus sagged against his side, limp and boneless, just as he'd obviously intended.

"What is it with you two guys, both kissing your

women in front of other people?" Chloe asked, looking back and forth between the brothers. "Ever hear of keeping it in the bedroom?"

Troy gave her an evil grin. "You've got a lot of room to talk, Miss After-Hours-in-the-Store."

Chloe glared. "All right, that's enough. How did you find out? I tortured Trent and he still swore it wasn't him. Did he really forget one of the cameras?"

Venus couldn't completely follow the conversation. But she did see the sparkle of satisfaction in Troy's eyes at his obvious attempt to get his brother in trouble with his wife.

Men. What totally strange creatures.

"I can't quite recall," Troy said with a deliberate shrug. "I thought for sure Trent had mentioned it."

"Bull." This from his brother, whose expression demanded his twin tell the truth. "Don't forget, paybacks are hell." He cast a knowing look toward Venus, as if warning Troy that he, too, now had a weak spot.

Never having considered herself anyone's weak spot before, Venus found herself liking the feeling.

"Oh, all right," Troy said with a phony-sounding sigh. "The security guard dropped some details about you paying him to leave for the night. I figured it out for myself." Glancing at Venus, he quickly explained about his brother's date with Chloe in the store after hours, concluding by saying, "He's such a cheapskate. Chloe, I'm amazed you ever went out with him again."

"He has his good points," Chloe said.

Troy glanced at Trent's clothes. "Obviously not when it comes to his wardrobe. I don't know which is worse," he said to Venus, "that you were kissing my brother, or that you mistook him for me to begin with. I wouldn't be caught dead in those jeans or work boots."

Trent snorted, staring pointedly at Troy's rumpled shorts and bare chest. "Oh, right, Mr. Style Plate. What's the matter, forget to forward your *GQ* subscription when you moved?"

Chloe raised a suggestive brow. "I don't know, honey. Your brother definitely has the legs for this look." Then she pursed her lips and gave a wolf whistle. "Not to mention the chest."

Troy smirked at his twin as Trent tightened his arm possessively. "Still playing the caveman, I see?"

Trent's gaze shifted to Venus, then back to Troy. "I'd better move over to make some room for you. Go ahead and grab a mastodon leg and sidle on up to the fire, little brother."

"Are they always like this?" Venus asked.

"Always," Chloe replied. "But if anyone else criticizes one of them you're in for a brawl."

Trent turned to his wife. "Damn straight. No one tells my brother he's a pompous, arrogant ass except me."

"And me," Venus quietly interjected.

"Oh, I knew I was going to like you," Chloe said with a grin. "You've looked past his hotshot facade though, haven't you? I hope so. Because there's something rather endearing about these two, in spite of the exterior package."

Venus gave Troy a long, assessing look, knowing the others could see her frank appreciation for his looks. "Can I admit I'm one shallow woman and have grown rather fond of the exterior package?"

Chloe gave Trent a look every bit as appreciative. "I guess that makes two of us."

Trent crossed his arms in front of his chest. "Now, are you going to apologize for believing I'd tell my brother about our date in the store? Are we finished with the cold shoulder?"

Troy looked truly amused. "You really got in trouble?"

Trent glared. "I had to take a day off and fly up here at the crack of dawn this morning with Chloe just to get this straightened out."

"Oh, baloney," Chloe said. She turned to Troy. "We came to meet Venus."

"Me? Why?"

"We've been waiting for this day," Chloe informed her. "I could hear in his voice that it had finally come. And getting a glimpse of this guy so jealous he could barely see straight? That was worth ten times what we paid in airfare. We wouldn't have missed this for the world."

Venus began to wonder if pregnancy affected the brain cells, because the woman wasn't making much sense. "Missed what?"

Chloe plopped into an overstuffed chair and lifted her feet onto a footrest. She crossed her arms over her swollen belly and stared at them, like someone waiting for a show to begin.

"Well, missed seeing some woman turn Troy into a complete driveling idiot. And here you are." Chloe nodded in satisfaction. "I'm so *very* happy to meet you."

WHEN TROY HAD PICTURED taking Venus to a theme park for the day, he'd imagined them holding hands, riding rides until they felt sick, eating a bunch of junk food and stealing hot, passionate kisses in dark tunnels. Lots of smiles. Lots of laughter. Lots of that wonderfully wicked attitude of hers.

He hadn't pictured his twin being in the third seat on every roller coaster, and his pregnant sister-in-law watching over them from any shady spot they could find for her.

Such was their day at Six Flags.

"A double date at a theme park," Venus said late in the afternoon. The four of them sat at an outdoor table, eating drippy ice cream. Chloe had to sample all their cones, insisting the baby hadn't yet decided what flavor was his or her favorite. "This is just so utterly..."

"Fabulous?" Chloe offered.

Trent sighed and two-pointed his balled-up napkin into a nearby trash can. "Sappy?"

Troy raised a brow. "Middle class?"

"I was going to say unexpected," Venus said with a chuckle as she gave Troy a light elbow to the ribs. "But how about we settle for all of the above?"

"I don't think we've double-dated since freshman year of college," Trent said. He shot Troy a taunting look. "Those blond twins in my lit 101 class."

Troy instantly knew what his brother meant. "Don't."

"I owe you for the store."

"Say one more word and I'll tell Chloe about Penny Marsden."

"Penny Marsden?" Chloe said, perking right up.

Trent groaned. "Jeez, that was eighth grade!"

"Good grief, Troy. Don't tell me Trent was as much of an early Don Juan as you," Venus muttered. "Two horny fourteen-year-old twins on the prowl? Your parents must have gone nuts."

Chloe sat up straight and put her hands flat on her belly, as if protecting the ears of her unborn child. "Fourteen?"

Trent looked like he wanted to reassure her, but Troy's confident smirk made him shut his mouth, just as he knew it would. His ten-minutes-older brother hated like hell to admit Troy had beat him at anything, including losing his virginity.

"Trent?" Chloe prompted.

"Aw, hell," his brother finally admitted. "So, for once, he did something first. I was sixteen."

"And a good thing, too," Venus said. "You were quite busy crashing cars, from what I hear. You didn't need the succession of women sneaking out of your room at night."

"Cars?" Chloe asked, fisting a hand and putting it on her hip. "As in *plural?*"

"From his street racing," Venus informed the other woman helpfully. Troy began to feel a hint of sympathy for his brother, who was going to have a really ticked-off, emotionally whacked-out pregnant woman to deal with when they got home.

This time Chloe almost snarled. "Street racing? Dammit, Trent Langtree, you said you never drove fast!"

"You're dead meat," Trent promised, looking ready to send some fists flying in Troy's direction for telling Venus about his wild teenage years.

"Venus," Troy asked, standing and tossing his napkin in the trash. "Care to risk death on the Superman ride again?"

Casting a quick, assessing look between Trent and Chloe, Venus nodded and leapt to her feet. "Less dangerous than here!"

Wrapping her fingers trustingly in his, she willingly followed him away from the other couple.

They spent the rest of the afternoon and early evening at the park, heading home at dusk. Troy couldn't remember when he'd had a better, happier, less stressful day.

It wasn't just being at a park designed for good times and fun. They'd all instantly taken to one another, and the four of them had spent most of the day in the kind of comfortable, friendly companionship which usually required years to cultivate. Trent and Chloe obviously really liked Venus. And she seemed to like them, too. She also seemed to like being away from the estate, able to be herself and not worry about wearing the right clothes or using the correct eating utensil.

The only serious moment came in the car when they were driving back to Max's estate late that night. "I'm so sorry we have to leave tonight on the red-eye," Chloe said. "I'd love to visit with you some more, Venus. Next time."

"Yes," Venus agreed. "You'll have to come up to Baltimore. We'll catch an Orioles game."

"Baltimore?" Trent said, looking surprised. "You're not staying in Atlanta?"

Troy tensed, waiting for her answer.

"No, of course not. This is just a vacation. A...trial run."

"But I thought you'd be staying here with your grandfather," Chloe continued. "He'd love that, I'm sure."

Beside her in the car, which they'd borrowed from Max for the drive to the park since his was too small, Troy waited to see what she'd say. They hadn't spoken about Venus's possible relationship to Max since the day she'd arrived, both seeming to want to take things as they came.

"I don't know how much Troy has told you," Venus explained.

"Not much," Troy assured her.

She took his hand, lacing her fingers with his on the vacant seat between them. "I don't honestly know if Max is my grandfather. You know, I suppose, about his son?"

Chloe didn't, but Trent and Troy told her about the

man's death. When they'd finished, she said, "So Leo has found some kind of evidence that made him believe you were Max Jr.'s long-lost baby, making you Mr. Longotti's granddaughter."

"Yes," Venus said. "But, to be honest, when I got here Monday, I truly didn't want him to be."

Just as Troy had suspected. He wondered if she'd explain why.

"Really?" Chloe asked, not pressing for more information.

Venus nodded. "It seemed easier to not believe it. You see, I've held on to this fantasy for a long time."

Trent leaned forward from the back seat, where he sat with his wife. "Fantasy?"

Venus's answering laughter was soft and sounded almost sad. "I've thought about my father since I was a little girl. Who he was, what he looked like, where he lives now. I guess I convinced myself that one day he was going to show up at my door, having just found out about me."

Troy tried to focus on the highway and not on the hint of hurt in the voice of someone he truly cared about.

"When Leo showed up at the bar last week with his crazy story, I...well, my first reaction was to wish I'd never laid eyes on him. I didn't want to believe it."

Troy was about to ask why she'd agreed to come to Atlanta with the man, if that were the case, but Chloe spoke first. "And now? Have you changed your mind? This morning, it seemed like you and Max were very close."

"He's great," Venus admitted. "I've never known anyone who could make me laugh so hard or who had more common sense. He's incredibly generous. And while he can be caustic and tough, he's much more vulnerable than he'd ever want anyone to realize."

Trent could sense her smile, though he couldn't see her face well in the shadowy confines of the car. "You love him," he stated, believing what he'd said, "even though you just met him."

She didn't deny it. "Max is a wonderful man. I wish I'd gotten to meet him long ago."

The woman had opened up her heart and let Max in after only a few days. She'd let her feelings for him ease into the empty part of herself that had been reserved for her lost father for decades. For all her toughness, Venus had again confirmed her innate sensitivity and capacity to care.

Troy had to ask. "So, Venus, if you've come to that realization...do you plan to stay? Permanently?"

After a long pause, when she glanced out the window to watch the approaching lights of oncoming cars, she softly murmured, "I honestly don't know, Troy."

He didn't lose heart—well, that wasn't correct since he suspected he'd already *lost* his heart. To her. But it was only Thursday night. He had three more days to change her mind.

Because, if he had his way, Venus wasn't going anywhere.

11

ON FRIDAY, Venus agreed to spend the entire day with Max. Troy had gone into the office early, saying he needed a day of work to recover from their trip to the theme park. Troy's teasing hadn't disguised his uncertainty. It had been evident since last night when he'd asked whether she'd be staying on in Atlanta. He hadn't asked her to. He'd said nothing to make her think he wanted her to, but she suspected he did.

How she could be so sure, she honestly couldn't say. She didn't delude herself that he'd fallen madly in love with her and couldn't bear for her to leave. They had a serious case of the hots going on. Their physical relationship was the most intense she'd experienced in her life. Venus wasn't ready for that to end any more than Troy seemed to be.

Late during the previous night, however, as she lay in his arms exchanging lazy kisses and whispers, she'd again acknowledged there was more than desire—on both their parts.

Guys who wanted only to nail a woman didn't typically introduce her to their families or take her on the floorless coaster over and over until they both thought they were going to be sick. Women who wanted only sex didn't automatically feel cherished because of the man's hand on her waist or his knowing smile.

He liked her as much as she liked him. With her track

record for dating losers, finding a man she just enjoyed being with—holding hands or sharing a cold bottle of water on a hot day—left her confused. She felt the way she had with Raul last year. Attraction had segued to liking. Then the realization that they could never have anything more permanent had made her walk away. She'd understood she couldn't risk losing her heart over someone moving in a different direction in his life.

Like Troy? Yeah. Like Troy.

Considering how soon she'd started feeling this way, she suspected Troy was a much bigger threat to her heart than Raul ever could have been. She'd *thought* she might eventually love Raul. She already *knew* she was falling in love with Troy. Not good when she was going back to Maryland in two days.

So stay here, a little voice told her.

A few days ago, she would have said no, absolutely not. Now she had to wonder. What was there to go back to in Baltimore? She had no job, not much of a home. Her friendships were strong enough to last in spite of distance and time between visits.

Max might well be her only living blood relative—a relative she'd liked on sight and now could honestly say she cared deeply about, as Troy had suggested last night. Max wasn't a young man. At times over the past few days he'd seemed tired and a bit confused, once even calling her Violet. Yesterday morning he'd mentioned Max Jr. being in the backyard playing ball, as if mixing up the events of the present with events forty years ago.

Who knew how long she'd have to enjoy him, her final connection to the father she'd never seen? If she left, she might be leaving behind much more than she'd ever expected to find when she'd boarded that plane from Baltimore on Monday morning.

As she walked outside to meet Max for breakfast, she paused in the doorway. He sat at a patio table beside the pool, sipping his tea, watching a pair of blue jays winging in and out of the leaves of a huge magnolia tree. Looking beyond him to the pool and the rolling lawn, she pictured what Max was seeing.

Max Jr.

On a sunny summer morning like this, he'd be swimming or perhaps playing baseball—breaking a window, getting scolded by his mother, and secretly praised for his swing by his father.

She could imagine him, visualize him, almost hear his voice. She was beginning to know him through Max's loving memories. Maybe in allowing *his* father into her heart, she'd be able to know her own father. And finally let the fantasy fade away.

Feeling more sure than she'd ever felt about anything, Venus walked to the table and kissed Max on the cheek. "Good morning."

Looking incredibly pleased, he took her hand. "Good morning to you. Ready for that shopping trip?"

Venus poured herself a glass of raspberry iced tea and shook her head. Then she told him what she wanted to do today.

He blinked twice, glancing down at his own clenched fingers. Max's voice shook slightly as he asked, "You're sure?"

Taking a deep breath, she nodded. "I am. If you don't mind, I'd really like to see some photos of Max Jr. and your wife."

He nodded again, still averting his gaze. As he reached for his cup, Venus touched his hand. When he looked up and met her stare, she saw moisture in his eyes. "And

Max, if it's all right with you, I'd like to go ahead and schedule that DNA test."

THE SUN WAS BRIGHT in her room the next morning when Venus awoke. She noticed one thing immediately—the weight of Troy's arm across her waist. "Troy, you overslept," she hissed, glancing toward her bedroom door.

Max might like the idea of her and Troy as a couple. He'd hinted at it again last night when the three of them had blown off the party and gone out to play miniature golf instead. But she didn't know how he'd feel about finding out they were already lovers...and had been since her second day in town!

She giggled, remembering how offended Max had been in the limo on the way to the party when she'd claimed golf was not a sport, but a way for rich guys to pretend to be athletic. Ordering the driver to detour to the nearest mini course, he'd challenged her to a game. Ten bucks a hole. He'd beaten the pants off her, as had Troy. But at least neither of them had collected on the bet.

Lying in Troy's arms, she still couldn't imagine what the other golfers—a mix of families with kids begging for tokens for the nearby video game, and teen couples on first dates—had thought of them. Two men in tuxes, her in the glorious red silk dress Troy had gotten for her, laughing as they argued their way through the course.

"What time...." Troy mumbled.

"It's after eight."

"Saturday," he replied, not even opening his eyes.

"Max's golf morning, which we know he takes very seriously. He could be knocking on my door to say goodbye at any moment."

That got his eyes open. He sat up in bed, giving her a quick good morning kiss and a slower goodbye one. "I think we need to stop sneaking around and come clean with Max," he whispered against her lips before finally pulling away to get out of bed.

"I know," she agreed. "But let's tell him, not *show* him." She couldn't resist casting an appreciative glance over his naked body. She sighed audibly, wanting him again already.

"Maybe I'd better take the back way out." He quickly donned a pair of briefs, which didn't fit well considering his body's reaction to her stare. "It would be bad enough running into anyone coming out of your room. I don't think there's any way I could hide *this.*"

"I'd love to help you *hide* it," she whispered with a saucy smile, eyeing the morning erection straining against the cotton.

"Oh, please," he said with an exaggerated rolling of the eyes. "Spare me the 'hide the salami' jokes, especially since you just kicked me out of your bed."

She lifted one shoulder, dropping the sheet lower until one breast was completely bared. "I didn't exactly kick you out..."

"Yeah, babe, you did, so don't go trying to tempt me back into it." He leaned down to give her one more hungry kiss and a playful stroke of her breast. She sighed and arched toward him, deepening the kiss, knowing she was tempting him to stay.

He finally pulled away with a groan and a softly muttered curse. "You're really bad," he said as he grabbed his clothes. "And damn, I'm crazy about you." Without another word after his shocking announcement, he grabbed his clothes. After crossing the room, he opened the person-high window. He waved and grinned his wicked, heartbreaking grin before ducking out onto the balcony connecting their two rooms.

After Troy left, Venus lay still for a full five minutes, thinking about what he'd said. Crazy about her, huh? She could live with that. For now, anyway.

A few moments later, she got up and showered. She spent several minutes under the pounding jets mentally reliving their long, sensual night. Finally, knowing she was going to get herself hopelessly aroused if she didn't knock it off, she forced herself to focus on something else. Like the previous day.

She and Max had spent hours going through album after album. She'd loved hearing every story as Max shared his memories of his family. Venus had never considered herself the emotional type. She didn't cry at weddings—except when she thought of the bucks the poor bride's parents had to put out for a one-day party with a bunch of near strangers too cheap to bring good gifts. Ditto on movies—with the exception of *Gone With The Wind*.

But seeing Max's life unfold on the pages of his albums, she'd cried. Particularly when gazing into the vivid green eyes of Violet Messina, and Max Jr. Those eyes, more than anything else, had convinced her she'd made the right decision about the DNA test. Staring into those photos had been like staring into a mirror.

At some point, while examining the photos, or perhaps while laughing nose to nose with Troy when he'd picked her up to swing her around after she'd made her one decent shot in mini golf, or maybe even twenty minutes ago when he'd told her he was crazy about her, she'd come to a decision.

She was staying in Atlanta. For herself. For Max.

And for Troy.

After drying off, she dressed and began to brush out her hair. When she heard a knock on her door, she figured Max was popping in. She was surprised to see Leo

Gallagher instead. "The prodigal nephew returns," she said. "I thought you were Max."

"I passed him downstairs as he left for his golf game."

Venus felt a twinge of disappointment that he hadn't stopped in for a morning chat. Continuing to brush her hair, she glanced at Leo and raised a brow. "You've been rather scarce."

"And you've been rather busy," he said, a small smile on his lips. The smile instantly put her on guard.

"What do you mean?"

"I noticed someone leaving through your window a little while ago when I pulled up."

Great. Leo had seen Troy. "I know we agreed on discreet..."

"Don't worry about it," he said. Not waiting for an invitation, he sat in a delicate antique chair in the corner. "I have to admit, with his reputation and your appearance, I rather suspected the two of you would...get along."

He didn't seem to mind. That bothered Venus more than anything else the man had said. It seemed so...un-Leo-like.

"So, you told Uncle Max you want the DNA test?"

She nodded warily. "Is that all right with you?"

Leo shrugged. "It's not necessary, but I have got someone lined up to take care of it."

Not entirely sure she wanted to know, she quietly asked, "Why is it not necessary, Leo?"

A slow satisfied smile crossed his lips. "Well, dear, because I have medical records listing your blood type and Max Jr.'s. I already know the truth. I've known all along."

She waited, her heart skipping a beat as she suddenly suspected what he was about to say.

"You are *not* Max Longotti's granddaughter."

As TROY SHOWERED, he wondered if Max had already stopped in to say goodbye to Venus. He hadn't heard the older man walking by his room, but suspected he wouldn't leave without a quick visit. Frankly, judging by the buoyant mood they'd both been in last night, he had a feeling the two of them had reached some kind of understanding about their relationship.

And that could mean Venus wasn't going home tomorrow.

He didn't stop to think too much about the big smile that possibility put on his face as he dried off and got dressed. He'd evaluate the feeling later, once he was sure she wasn't flying out of his life within twenty-four hours.

Wanting to see her again already, but not wanting to interrupt if she was with Max, he decided to visit her the same way he'd left. He opened his window and stepped out onto the balcony. The curtains flowing in the gentle morning breeze told him her window was still open as well.

As he approached, he was easily able to distinguish two voices—Venus's and a man's. Assuming she was with Max, he decided to leave them alone. Then he paused, hearing a word sounding like the kind often used by sailors.

It had been spoken by Venus.

"You selfish bastard," she continued, sounding furious.

"Don't take the high road," the man replied.

Troy recognized the voice of Leo Gallagher. Leaning closer, he saw the other man sitting stiffly in Venus's room.

"You can't tell me you don't want the money."

"I *don't* want the money," she snapped.

Money? Troy's jaw tightened.

"You wanted it a week ago, didn't you? You were quick enough to cash my check and come down here, even though you didn't believe what I'd told you was true."

"Shows how right my instincts were," Venus said. Troy couldn't see her—she obviously stood in a corner near the bathroom, out of his range of sight. "I can't believe you knew all along I couldn't be Max Jr.'s daughter and did this anyway. Or that I was stupid enough to cash your check."

Troy drew in a deep breath, shaking his head as a wave of disappointment washed over him. Venus had been paid to come here. No matter how angry she was at Leo now, she'd accepted his money to meet Max. Troy couldn't help feeling betrayed. Not so much because she'd done it but because she'd been lying about it. In spite of what had happened between them, she hadn't trusted him enough to come clean.

"Get out, Leo. I'm packing up and going home. I will not be used by you so you can get your grubby hands on Max's business."

The man didn't seem concerned. "Be sure to tell him goodbye before you leave."

"You bet I will." Her words were almost snarled. "I'll be sure to tell him all about his loyal nephew, who brought me down here to try to run a scam. What did you think, that you'd talk me into convincing him not to sell to Troy's family?"

Troy wondered the same thing. He frankly couldn't see what Leo had to gain out of this whole scheme, with the exception of time. A DNA test would have proven the truth, and Max would still have sold. It just might have taken longer.

"That was one option," Leo said. "It still can be, if you

stop and think of the money you could make. I have someone lined up to run the DNA test in our favor. You can stay and live happily as Max's granddaughter. Make him happier than he's been in years." Though he was obviously trying to appear concerned, he was unable to hide the note of self-satisfaction in his voice.

"The two of you can be together and you can convince Max to retire, keeping the company in the family—with me at the helm."

"What was the other option?" Venus asked, sounding weary.

Leo appeared to visibly relax, and Troy wondered if something in Venus's expression had led him to think he was getting through to her.

The man obviously didn't know who he was dealing with.

"Many people know about Max's medical problems, including the board of Longotti Lines." Leo stood and approached the window, though not coming close enough to see Troy outside. "He's also not in the best emotional shape. But he's grown very fond of you, hasn't he? Pinned all his hopes and dreams on your pretty shoulders. Finding out you're not his little Violet, such a severe disappointment...well, he could break down. *Again.*"

Troy closed his eyes briefly, remembering what Mrs. Harris had let slip the other evening about Max's previous breakdown. His fingers clenched into fists and he wanted nothing more than to slam them into Leo Gallagher's self-serving face.

"You cruel man." Venus's voice was low and thick with emotion. Troy knew her well enough by now to recognize the fury buried in the sadness. "I have to say, in spite of the things I've seen in my life, I can still be surprised by how damn vicious some people can be."

Leo continued as if she hadn't spoken. "I don't think I'll have much problem convincing the voting board members Max isn't competent to make major decisions about the future of the company." He shrugged in satisfaction. "So, you see Ms. Messina, either way, I'll get what I want. All that remains to be seen is whether you care enough to keep an old man happy in his final years. Or if you prefer to tell him the truth and make him fall apart, after which I'll step in and take over the company anyway."

"I won't lie to a man who's been nothing but kind to me."

"Suit yourself," Leo replied. "By all means, tell him the truth. Might be quicker that way." He stood and plucked an invisible piece of lint off his navy sport jacket, still seeming perfectly content with the way his plan had progressed.

"You won't get away with it, Leo. I'll tell the board what you did," she said, her voice regaining its steely tone.

Leo chuckled. "Who would believe you? I have the cancelled check you cashed. I was your dupe, the pawn of a grubby foster kid turned bartender who tried to con us all. Poor Uncle Max."

Troy had heard enough. Pushing through the billowing curtains, he entered Venus's bedroom and strode across the room. He grabbed Leo by the collar of his designer jacket.

"Langtree!"

"They'll believe her," Troy snarled. "Because I heard every miserable word, you lousy little prick."

Before Leo could respond, before Troy could even give

the man a good hard shake, the bedroom door was pushed in from the hall. "As did I."

Venus, who still couldn't quite believe Troy had just stalked in here like an avenging god, watched in dismay as Max entered, looking pale and shaken. And very, very angry.

"Max, how long have you been standing there?" She went to his side to take his arm.

He patted her hand. "Long enough. Don't worry, dear. I'm fine." He turned to his nephew. "Get out of my house. Remove your belongings from my offices. With four witnesses, I think we'll be able to convince the board that you're completely unsuitable for any type of responsible position."

Venus followed Max's glance toward the doorway, seeing Mrs. Harris standing there. She'd obviously heard every word, too.

"Uncle Max, I..." Leo attempted.

Max held up a steady, unshaking hand, silently ordering him to stop. "Out. Right now, before I call the police."

Obviously knowing he couldn't twist this situation to suit himself, Leo cast a glare at Venus. He swept out of the room, brushing past Mrs. Harris. The housekeeper turned to follow him, her arms crossed over her chest. She appeared to want to ensure Leo didn't pick up any souvenirs as he left.

When the three of them were alone in the room, Venus slid her arm around Max's waist. "I feel so awful."

"None of this was your fault, Venus. You were used as much as I was by the slimy weasel. I'm so glad we're not actually blood relatives. Never could stand the little peckerwood."

Venus bit the corner of her lip.

"I was this close to introducing him to my fist," Troy

said. "I don't think I've ever felt such violence toward anyone in my life."

"Just as well you didn't," Max replied succinctly. "He'd have found the nearest ambulance chaser and sued you but good."

Seeing the man trying so hard to joke, to reassure her, Venus felt tears rise in her eyes. "I'm so sorry, Max." He shrugged, obviously about to tell her again it wasn't her fault. She hurried to explain. "What I mean is, I'm so sorry I'm not *her*." Her voice broke and she cleared her throat. "I wish more than anything that I was really your granddaughter."

"So do I, honey," he murmured, still patting her hand. "Can I confess that in my heart, you always will be?"

Troy edged toward the door, probably thinking they wanted to be alone. "I think I'd better go down to the office and make some phone calls. Leo's going to try to twist this his way and we need to cut his legs out from under him right up front."

"Let me start here at the house with some of the long-standing members of the board," Max said. He glanced back and forth between Venus and Troy. "I should go downstairs now and make sure Mrs. Harris isn't having any trouble with Leo. Troy, I'll see you shortly?" Before he left, he pressed a kiss to Venus's temple. "Come visit me later, when you're feeling better, all right? We'll talk things over."

She nodded, blinking rapidly. She didn't want him to see her cry, not when he'd been so strong. As soon as he was out of the room, with the door shut behind her, however, she felt the moisture on her cheeks.

Without a word, Troy pulled her into his arms, twisting his fingers into her hair to cup her head and hold her tight. "It's all right," he whispered. "Max is going to be okay. Leo didn't give him enough credit—he's a tough old guy."

She let the tears come, crying for Max. For herself. For the fantasy father she'd let go of while she'd tried to embrace an unexpected gift of family. Now that family had been yanked away too, leaving her with nothing.

Though she was glad she'd gotten to meet Max, part of her wished she'd never come. Once again, love seemed to be a blessing and a curse. She'd begun to love the old man. And, like nearly everyone else she'd ever loved, she'd lost him. At this moment, she couldn't say whether the emotion was worth the heartache.

Troy tugged her down to sit beside him on the bed. She kept her face buried in his neck, sucking up his comfort and warmth like a kid burrowing into a parent.

"Venus, baby, don't," he whispered, stroking her hair, her back, and kissing her temple. "Max doesn't blame you."

"He should. I should have trusted my instincts about Leo."

He shook his head, and finally Venus took a deep breath and pulled away. They remained on the bed, face-to-face. Troy looked concerned and understanding, but she thought there was also a hint of something else in his eyes. It was as if a veil had dropped over them and just a bit of the warmth with which he'd looked at her before had been lost.

"Did you hear everything?" she asked.

He nodded. "I knew Leo had you all wrong and you wouldn't do it. Once you began to love Max, you couldn't have betrayed him."

Though his trust warmed her, she again noted something remaining unsaid. Then she began to understand. "But before I got to know him...I took Leo's money."

Troy stiffened so slightly, she almost wondered if she imagined it. But she knew she hadn't.

"Max isn't angry about the money."

"You are."

He didn't answer with words. His eyes were telling enough.

"I shouldn't have lied about it," she admitted.

"I wish you hadn't. I'd hoped you'd started to trust me enough to tell me the truth."

She glanced away. "I guess I'm not used to trusting people."

"Me, neither," he admitted with a rueful sigh.

"Maybe that's why we got along so well from the start." She paused. "And why it's best for me to leave now."

"You don't have to go," he said. "You heard Max—he doesn't blame you. He cares about you. He'd be glad if you stayed."

She waited for a few seconds—the length of a heartbeat—for Troy to continue. Would he admit he cared for her, too? Did *he* want her to stay? When he said nothing, she sat up straighter, more resolved. "I was leaving tomorrow anyway." Her voice didn't catch at all on the lie. "I'll stay in touch with Max."

He raised a brow, waiting for her to continue. When she didn't, he said, "And me? Will you stay in touch with me, Venus?"

Would she? Could they maintain a long-distance affair, with occasional trips for hot, exciting weekends filled with passion and laughter? A day or two ago, she might have said yes. But that was before. Before she'd realized she was in love with him. Before she'd been reminded just how heart wrenching love could be.

If she really thought they had a future, she might have

risked it. But they didn't. She was *not* the long-lost heir to a millionaire. She was not going to be living in an Atlanta mansion, mingling with the kind of polite society Troy was used to. She was the one who couldn't dance, had wild taste in clothes and didn't know one utensil from another. She was the unemployed, broke bartender from Baltimore with a mountain of debt and a string of bad relationships trailing along behind her.

I'm the woman who took money from a stranger to come play on the hopes of a sad, heartbroken old man.

The memory shamed her. How could Troy not be ashamed of her, too? She'd seen that look in his eyes. She knew he no longer trusted her. They wouldn't end up together in the long run. So, for her own protection, she needed to walk away now.

"I don't think so, Troy. This has been amazing. But we both knew it was short-term. Lust. Not...not love. We're too different for it to be anything more than physical. And physical seldom survives long distances." She forced a humorless laugh. "Out of sight, out of mind, as they say."

His jaw stiffened and intensity flashed in his eyes. "I don't think I'll ever get you out of my mind, and I don't want to try." He lifted a brow in that confident, sexy expression of his. "Have you forgotten? I agree with you about Rhett and Scarlett. Insanity is better than boredom any day. Opposites attract, but don't stay together. Like belongs with like, Venus."

She almost smiled, knowing he still wanted her, knowing she felt the same way. He just hadn't yet seen the flaw in his logic.

"Don't you see, Troy?" she asked softly, admitting the truth to herself, as much as to him. "We *are* opposites."

If this were really *Gone With The Wind*, he'd be Rhett

and she'd be Belle Watling, the madame with the heart of gold who could never fit into the hero's rich highbrow world.

She'd thought they were alike, and perhaps in some ways, they were. But not enough for forever. Not enough to prevent eventual heartache.

He opened his mouth to reply, but before he could say a word, the door opened and Mrs. Harris looked in. "Mr. Longotti thinks you should come down now," she said to Troy, giving them both a sorrowful look. "Apparently Mr. Gallagher has been making some calls on his cellular phone already. Mr. Longotti doesn't have the numbers for all the board members here at the house and thinks you should go into the office right away."

Troy looked torn. Finally he stood. "This isn't finished, Venus. We'll talk about it later, when I get back, all right?"

Later, when he got back, she intended to be gone. But she didn't say anything.

Troy turned to follow Mrs. Harris out. Before exiting the room, however, he turned back to the bed. Cupping her cheek in his hand, he tilted her face up and pressed a hard, insistent kiss on her mouth. "This conversation isn't over."

She had to disagree. Two hours later, after a heartfelt goodbye to Max, who tried to convince her to stay, Venus got in a cab for the airport. As she flew away from Atlanta, she whispered, "You're wrong, Troy. It's definitely over."

12

VENUS SPENT her first two days back in Baltimore wallowing and eating lots of chocolate. Max called twice, both times telling her she was always welcome in his home. He'd also mentioned Troy. "He's angry, and, I think, hurt," Max said Sunday night. "He can't understand why you left. I can't either. I have eyes—I know something happened between you two."

Knowing Max was only trying to be helpful, she admitted the truth. "He thinks we're a lot alike. I think we're opposites. Maybe it wouldn't matter if we were both a little right, or both a little wrong, *if* we really loved each other."

At her pause, Max prompted, "And you don't?"

She couldn't answer. Instead, she changed the subject, making Max chuckle while she told him stories of her moody cat, who'd repaid her for being gone by leaving yucky presents all over her apartment her first day back.

He *hadn't* laughed when she'd told him someone had broken into the vestibule of her apartment building twice last week, vandalizing the mail boxes. Luckily, Venus had arranged to have her mail held before she left, meaning there'd be a bunch of bills to pick up at the post office Monday morning.

"Funny," Max said. "It turns out Leo was in Baltimore last week, while you were here. He was meeting with a P.I., whose name has turned up on some checks from

Longotti Lines over the years." He sniffed. "My accountants spent the day in the office. They think the sneaky little bastard's a thief as well as a liar."

Venus's first thought was to wonder if Leo had thought to steal his money back from her. She thrust it out of her mind—Leo had told her he had the cancelled check, so he knew she'd cashed it. She had absolutely nothing else that he needed, and he'd only known about her for a matter of weeks. So the P.I. had to have been working on something else that didn't involve her.

The pile of bills at the post office was bigger than she'd feared, so Monday she went straight to Flanagan's. She needed money. Since she'd sent the entire five thousand dollars she'd gotten from lousy Leo to her foster mother—unable to even consider keeping a dime of it for herself—she needed cash *now*.

"Tell you what," Joe said when she showed up. "You tell me where I can find this Leo guy so's I can break both his legs, and you can come back to work right now."

Venus kissed his grizzled cheek and got to work.

On Wednesday afternoon, Joe's waitress had an appointment and Venus leapt at the chance for an extra shift. Wednesdays were the slowest day at Flanagan's, so after lunch Venus assured Joe she could handle things while he ran to the bank. He'd been worried about keeping cash on hand because of a rough-looking stranger who'd hung around a lot last week.

"Hey," he said before leaving, "I forgot. There's a package for you. Maureen sent it here since she knew you were away. It's under the bar."

Remembering her foster mother had promised to send some old papers, Venus glanced at the package. Not wanting to open it until she was alone, she left it on the shelf.

Right now, two businessmen occupied a corner booth. When they weren't hitting on her, they were busy whispering, probably about their plans for world domination, or for screwing over their shareholders. An elderly woman and her two middle-aged daughters, who said they were on a shopping spree, were in another booth.

The only other person in the place was a silent, dark-haired chick dressed all in black, who sat at the bar. She faced the door, able to see everyone who entered. Venus had the feeling she didn't trust anyone enough to present them with her back. With her pale skin, striking hair, dark clothes and unsmiling expression, she reminded Venus of Tuesday Adams from the old Adam's Family show.

None of them were conversationalists, which left Venus time to wallow in self-pity because she hadn't heard from Troy. She shouldn't have cared—she was the one who'd left without a goodbye. But, dammit, he could have at least made the effort.

"Probably moved on to the next willing female before my plane left the ground," she muttered.

Taking a damp rag to a stubborn dried stain on the surface of the bar, she glanced up when the door opened. About two grand worth of designer clothes, wrapped around a stunning redhead, walked in off the street. A lifetime worth of antipathy for the wealthy sent a tiny shot of stiffness up her spine.

Then Venus paused. She'd just spent a week with a rich man, Max, whom she now truly loved. Besides, this woman had a simmering look of intrigue and a boatload of attitude. That made anyone okay in Venus's book. She greeted the newcomer with a smile.

"Cool shirt," the woman said. She took a seat at the bar, crossing her legs in a way that most women in a short dress would consider a requisite for modesty, but which Venus recognized as a subtle sign to any man within drooling distance. A glance at the dweebs in the booth confirmed the Pavlovian response.

Venus looked down at her favorite old T-shirt, complete with saucy mascot. Troy might not have known who she was, but any self-respecting redhead sure as hell would. She grinned, then glanced at the other woman's designer outfit. "You don't look like the T-shirt type."

The woman's warm laugh continued to draw the eyes of the two businessmen, as she'd almost certainly intended, probably more due to nature than design. "Believe me, sister, I don't dress this way every day. And I certainly don't do it for myself."

Frankly, if Venus had buckets of money, she'd dress *only* to please herself. Except, perhaps, in the bedroom. Hell, for Troy, she might actually have given in and tried a thong again!

The woman had continued speaking, still talking about Venus's shirt and Jessica Rabbit. "I'd like to think I have a lot in common with her. Not bad, just drawn that way."

Venus nodded. "Ditto." Without being told, she instinctively knew the woman with the smoky voice would be a whiskey drinker. She poured her a shot of the good stuff and slid it over. "My name's Venus. Venus Messina."

The woman extended her hand. "Sydney. Sydney Colburn."

Venus instantly recognized the name, which was on the spine of several of her all-time favorite novels. "Sydney Colburn. No kidding? The writer?"

After Sydney tasted the whiskey, she nodded that it was to her liking. "One and the same."

Sydney Colburn's books had provided many nights' escape during the past year. Venus might have sworn off men physically, but she'd been addicted to reading about the kind of fabulous guys this woman created with such thrilling—*throbbing*—detail.

After telling Sydney how much she'd liked her heroes, saying it was too bad more men couldn't live up to her standard, she added, "And my favorite thing about your books—no wimpy heroines!"

"Men who meet my standard do exist," the author said softly. "The trouble is finding them."

Venus almost snorted at that one. "Finding men has never been a problem for me." Hell, she'd been finding men who'd attracted her since she had been old enough to look up the word orgasm in the dictionary! "Keeping them? That's another story."

"The good ones or the so-so ones?"

Venus sighed. "Good or even so-so wouldn't be bad. Unfortunately, the only ones I seem to manage to hang on to are the creeps who cost you jobs or empty your bank accounts. Not the green-eyed dreamboats with chestnut hair and the kind of wicked, sexy grin that oughta be illegal." She glanced away, trying to thrust Troy's image out of her mind.

Sydney obviously noticed and made a knowing sound. "What?"

"You got it bad, sister."

Venus scowled. "Speak for yourself."

After Sydney admitted she *was* speaking for herself, Venus poured her another drink.

"We bad girls have it tough, you know?" Venus said. "Those Goody Two-shoes have saying 'no' down to an art form, blaming morals or past hurts. We say yes because of those *same* morals or past hurts! We can't seem to give up on the idea that the next handsome stud who comes along might erase what the last one did."

"Handsome studs are a dime a dozen."

The lady in black, whom Venus had nearly forgotten about, had obviously been following their conversation. Venus approached the attractive young woman, whose demeanor, clothes and attitude sent off one signal: mysterious. "Hey, girl, I almost forgot you were here. Come join us. Bad girls need to stick together."

The woman looked back and forth between them, still wary, but considering. Then her lip curled, possibly in jaded amusement. "Bad girls. Are we forming a club here?"

Venus snorted at the very idea. "Last club I belonged to was the Girl Scouts. I got kicked out when I was eleven." As Sydney raised a questioning brow, Venus explained. "Summer camp. I got caught sneaking into the boys' cabin to play Seven Minutes in Heaven. The troop leader came in just as I was heading into the closet with Tommy Callahan." She shook her head and sighed at the memory. "He had the cutest dimples. And cool braces."

Sydney nodded, wearing a similar look of reminiscence.

A grin suddenly brightened the features of the woman in black, softening her face and making her look younger than Venus had figured her to be. "I never made it past Brownies. I kept altering the uniform in a way that, well, didn't meet with the troop leader's approval. But the boys liked it." She winked. "Besides, brown isn't my color."

"Hell," Sydney proclaimed, "my mother never let me forget I got tossed outta preschool for showing the boys my underwear."

Venus snickered. "Hey, why was she complaining?"

"Yeah," the brunette said with a knowing look at Venus. They finished the thought in unison. "At least you were wearing 'em."

The three of them, strangers until ten minutes before, but sisters just the same, shared a moment of soft laughter. Seeing the understanding in their eyes, Venus wished she'd met them long ago. "I guess we've been members of the bad girls club since birth, huh?"

Sydney silently lifted her glass in salute, and the other woman followed suit. Venus popped the cap off a beer and joined them in an unspoken toast to wicked women everywhere. *God love them.*

The door opened again. This time, two young women in proper business attire entered to join the men in the booth. The suit-clad oglers promptly sat up straighter. "Oh, no, a good girl's in sight, reign in the lust," Venus whispered.

The stranger in black picked up her drink and moved next to Sydney, introducing herself as Nicole Bennett. They chatted for several more minutes, until the ring of Sydney's cell phone interrupted.

Venus left to wait on the two newcomers—white wine spritzers, she coulda predicted that a mile away—then returned to find Sydney disconnecting her call. The woman drained her glass and dropped a bill on the counter. When Venus realized it was a hundred, she picked it up. "I'll get your change."

Sydney, however, refused. She ordered Venus to keep the change and get Nicole good and drunk. Then, with a cheery wave, she walked toward the door, easily moving out of Venus's life as quickly as she'd moved into it.

Or, not so easily, considering her way out the door was blocked by someone coming in. A man. A big man. A big chestnut-haired man with the kind of sexy grin that oughta be illegal.

Troy.

TROY WAITED for the jolt of awareness that always shot through his body when an attractive female passed by. The redhead exiting Flanagan's bar was certainly attractive—and knew it—but caused no familiar blast of heat to rush through him.

Only one woman did that now. The one standing behind the bar, looking ready to do one of two things: slug him, or jump on him. "Hi, Venus."

"What are you doing here?"

"I'm thirsty," he said as he slid onto a bar stool and tapped his fingers on the pitted wood surface of the bar. "What do you recommend? A Screaming Orgasm? Sex on the Beach?"

She smirked. "A Screaming Orgasm Up Against the Wall is always a good choice."

He swallowed, hard. Damn, he'd missed the woman. "How about a Screaming Orgasm Up Against the Bathroom Counter? Or In the Pool?" His grin dared her to remember. Before she could say a word, however, they both heard a tiny wolf whistle from a dark-haired woman sitting at the bar. Troy had barely noticed her, though she was striking enough to garner attention on her own.

"Yep. Definitely oughta be illegal." She nodded at Venus, then walked out.

"Who was that?"

"A new friend," Venus said softly. "Now, why are you here?"

He answered with a question of his own. "Why did you leave?"

She busied herself pouring some unshelled peanuts into a wooden bowl. "What was the point of staying?"

"Maybe because Max wanted you to?" When she didn't answer, he leaned closer. "Okay, how about because *I* wanted you to?"

She paused, not meeting his eye. "Did you want me to? Why?"

He sighed, wondering how such an intelligent woman could be so blind to her own appeal. Finally, tired of watching her pretend to swipe at the counter with her dingy rag, he grabbed her hand and made her stop. Then he waited until she met his eye. "Yes, I wanted you to. I told you I'm crazy about you."

Her eyes narrowed. "That's nice. But I have my own life, back here. We knew I was going to have to leave sooner or later."

"You could have stayed in Atlanta. With Max." He hesitated, then pushed harder, wondering if she was any more ready to hear this than he was ready to say it. "Or with me."

She raised a questioning brow. "You?"

"I moved into my own place Monday, between meetings with lawyers, the board and a P.I. It's downtown, near a Marta stop and some great shopping." He glanced around the pub and continued to try to tempt her. "There's even an Irish bar."

She nibbled one corner of her lip, moistening it with the tip of her pretty pink tongue. "You want me to live with you?"

He nodded. "There. Or here. I told Max I might be resigning from my job. It all depends on you."

"Because...you're crazy about me?"

Hell, he'd already gone farther with Venus than he'd ever gone with any woman—asking her to move in. Having gone this far, he figured he might as well jump in feet first. Leaning across the bar, with his elbows on the wood, he tugged her other hand in his and pulled her closer. "Because I'm in love with you, Venus."

She yanked her hands back. "Get *out!* You are *so* not in love with me."

Not quite the reaction he'd hoped for the first time he told a woman he loved her. He grinned. Maybe that was why he'd fallen in love with her in the first place. "No lie, babe. It's love."

"You can't love me."

He didn't know who she was trying to convince, but it sure wasn't going to be him. "I do."

"We're too different."

"No, we're not. We're the same."

She flung the rag down and crossed her arms in front of her chest. "No, we're not the same. A guy can be a total dog and still be a wealthy, respected businessman. A woman makes a few...dozen...mistakes, and she's a bad girl for life."

He snickered. God, she was just priceless.

Troy saw that they'd drawn the attention of the other people in the place, including two couples who'd walked in behind him. But he didn't give a damn. "Venus, we're a hell of a lot alike in every way that really matters. Besides, honey, you are not nearly as bad as you like to pretend."

Her spine stiffened at the tossed gauntlet. "I seduced my dentist when I was nineteen."

Okay. One-upmanship. He could handle that. "I slept with the mother of one of my college buddies when I was nineteen."

Her eyes narrowed. "I did it to get out of paying for a crown."

"I did it to get laid."

She glared, then thought about it. "I flashed the boy's

soccer team from the top of the bleachers when I was a freshman."

"Did they win the game?"

She rolled her eyes.

"I had the entire senior cheerleading squad at each other's throats before soccer season even started because I'd been dating four of them at the same time," Troy admitted.

She harrumphed. "I started sneaking out with guys before I'd even hit puberty."

He chuckled. "I think we already discussed this. I didn't have to sneak *out*, because I was too busy sneaking females *in*."

An elderly woman, sitting in a booth nearby with two middle-aged ladies, tittered. "Sounds like you two are made for each other."

Troy gave her a quick smile of thanks. "I agree."

Venus still didn't look convinced. "So we were both rotten little sex fiends. That's not all." She began to tick off her fingers, cataloguing her badness. "I refuse to pay parking tickets. My picture's on a wanted poster at the library because I return books so late. And," she continued, dramatically slapping her hand on the surface of the bar, "I quite often have more than ten items at the express checkout at the grocery store."

"I hate it when people do that," the old lady muttered.

Troy took her hand again. "I love you."

"You can't."

"I *do*."

She lowered her eyes, until her lashes brushed the curves of her lovely cheeks. When she looked up again, her green eyes were suspiciously bright. "I took money from Leo to come to Atlanta, never even stopping to think I might be hurting a wonderful old man who'd never done a thing to me."

He understood. Finally, he understood. Not answering, Troy walked around the bar, pushing through a swinging half door designed to keep customers away. Venus watched him, wide-eyed, backing up until she was blocked by a huge silver vat of beer.

"You didn't keep the money, did you." It wasn't a question. He knew without asking what her answer would be.

She shook her head slowly. "I sent it to my foster mother. How did you know?"

He brushed a long tendril of red hair off her brow, gently tucking it behind her ear. Lightly caressing her earlobe, he then ran his fingers across her jaw, down her neck, until his hand rested on her strong, stubborn shoulder. "Because I know you, Venus Messina. You're honorable. You're honest." He leaned closer, inhaling to breathe in the sweetness of her cinnamon-tinged perfume. "And you're too damn good for me."

She tried to shake her head in denial, but he caught her chin and held her still. "You're too good for me," he repeated. "I don't deserve you. But the truth is, I'm a selfish enough bastard to want you anyway."

Not giving her another chance to throw up any more ridiculous obstacles, he pulled her close and pressed a sweet, gentle kiss on her lips. She softened in his arms, returning his kiss, then pulled back.

"We're still opposites," she whispered, stubborn to the last. Studying him from head to toe, she rolled her eyes. "Look at us." She pointed down to her tight-as-sin jeans and sexy-as-hell T-shirt. "I'm a walking advertisement for a thrift shop. And there you are in your designer shirt and pants that probably cost more than I paid for my couch."

"I can take off the shirt," he said, reaching for the top button, letting her see the mischievous look in his eye.

She glanced at the bar crowd. "Oh, yeah, right."

"You think I won't?"

"Maybe you want me to think you will," she taunted.

He slipped the button free. She kept watching, silently egging him on, never moving her gaze away from him as he slowly unfastened every single button. He tugged the shirt free of his waistband and shrugged it off his shoulders, dropping it to the floor. He knew every person in the place was watching them, him, standing shirtless behind the bar, but he didn't care. Venus, with her hot, devouring eyes, was all he cared about.

"You didn't think I'd do it."

A wicked smile widened her beautiful lips. She tapped his chest with the tip of her index finger, until he was the one backing up. "Oh, I knew you'd do it, Troy. Why else do you think I suggested it?"

He turned the tables on her, picking her up by the waist and turning around to deposit her on top of the bar. Then he stepped easily between her long, jean-clad legs and tugged her closer, until her parted thighs rested on his hips. He ignored the flurry of whispers and a definite sigh or two from the women seated in the place. "Tell me you love me."

She continued to stare at him, both amusement and sensual awareness in her eyes.

He pulled her closer, feeling the warm dampness of her jeans against his stomach. Sliding his hands up under the bottom of her shirt, he caressed her waist, then reached around to stroke the delicate bones of her spine. Leaning forward, he pressed a hot, moist kiss in the hollow of her throat. "I won't stop until you tell me," he threatened.

She dropped her head back and moaned. "I won't tell you if you stop."

"I'd tell him absolutely *anything*," a woman's voice said in a loud whisper.

They both began to laugh and finally Venus took pity. Her brilliant emerald eyes glittered with happiness as she dropped her arms over his shoulders and met his unflinching stare.

"I love you, Troy." She leaned down to kiss him, parting her lips to let him sample the sweetness of her mouth. She sighed as their kiss ended, and whispered, "Now, take me home."

"To Atlanta?"

She shook her head. "No way can I make it to Atlanta today. We'll go tomorrow. But when my uncle gets back, you can take me to my apartment before I rip off the rest of your clothes and get us both arrested."

THAT EVENING in her apartment, after three solid hours of the most incredible lovemaking of her life, Venus asked Troy to fill her in on what had been happening in Atlanta. "Max sounds okay. Is he going to be able to keep Leo in line?"

Troy grabbed another egg roll from the mountain of carry-out spread all over the coffee table in her living room. "Yeah. Max has got enough on Leo to force him out of the company and he could press criminal charges if he wanted to. But I still can't help wondering what Leo's been up to with this P.I. in Baltimore."

Feeling a little silly about it, Venus admitted her earlier suspicion. "If I had anything worth stealing, I might have wondered if he was responsible for the mail thefts."

"Wait a second," Troy said, casting a quick glance toward the door, where they'd dropped their clothes, her purse, and the package she'd brought home from Flanagan's. "You said that box was delivered to you at the bar last week, right? And your uncle Joe was worried about some shady character hanging around?"

It sounded crazy. "It was just a bunch of paperwork from my foster mother. You don't think..."

He glanced again toward the door. Finally, curious herself, Venus got up and brought the shoe-box-size package to the table. She tore off the brown paper, then removed the lid. A note rested inside. "From Maureen," she said as she scanned it. "She said most of her paperwork was taken in the robbery when I was in high school. But DCF sent these things to me at her place after my eighteenth birthday. I'd already come to Baltimore. She told me she had it ages ago, but I completely forgot."

Troy looked at the pile of papers, and a small red leather-bound book. "A diary?"

Venus recognized the book. "My mother's. I didn't know what had happened to it. I guess the state kept everything for me until I was of legal age, since no other family came forward."

"Maybe you should read it later," he said, a look of intense concern on his face.

Knowing she might regret it, she reached for the diary, anyway. She trusted Troy more than she'd ever trusted anyone in her life. And if reading her mother's words was going to be painful for her, she could think of no one better to be right beside her, holding her hand, than the man she loved.

An open envelope containing some legal-looking papers was stuck to the book. As she retrieved it, the papers fell out, fluttering to the floor beside Troy. Focused on the diary, she barely paid attention as he reached for them to put them back.

Just as she opened the faded, aged cover of the diary, she heard Troy make a strange confused sound. She barely had time to register what was taped on the inside cover of the diary—a strip of photos, like those taken at photography booths in the mall—when she heard him say, "Oh, my God."

"What's the matter, Troy?"

His eyes were wide with shock. "Honey, Venus..."

"What is it?"

"I was trying to fold them to put them back," he explained, as if he feared she'd think he was snooping.

She glanced at the legal document in his hand. "What is it?"

He handed it to her. But before she even glanced at it, she felt a strange tingling of something in her spine. Recognition. Culmination. Understanding. Because in that brief glimpse at the photo strip in her mother's diary, she'd seen a face she'd never expected to see.

Letting the document fall to her lap, she opened the book again and looked at the photographs. Her mother's smiling face was easily recognizable...as was the face of the laughing man, mugging it up for the camera beside Trina.

Max Longotti Jr.

She knew it was him. She'd seen enough pictures of the handsome young man at Max's place the week before to instantly know the thick dark hair, the green eyes, the dimple in his left cheek.

Tears spilled out of her eyes.

Troy shoved the table out of the way, ignoring the cartons of food tumbling onto the floor. He pulled her into his arms. "It's all right, Venus. It's okay," he murmured as he stroked her back.

"It's Max Jr." She felt numb and almost couldn't grasp the words she spoke. "In the photos. With my mother. It's him."

"I know." Troy kissed her brow. "The paper was a registered document showing your name was legally changed to Venus when you were two years old." He held her tighter. "From Violet."

She closed her eyes, letting it sink in, accepting the truth. Trina really had met and loved Max Longotti Jr. Even without reading the diary, she understood what had happened. Their whirlwind love affair. Trina's inability to contact the mysterious "Matt" after he'd gone off to California. Her birth. His death. Years of not knowing. Finally Trina losing hope and changing Venus's first name, but not having the heart to go that final step and change the last one.

She understood just about everything. "Leo..."

"I'm gonna kill that son of a bitch," Troy muttered.

"He's known for a long time, I suspect."

Troy nodded. "Probably for years. I imagine he kept it from everyone, not wanting you found. Then I came along. He started worrying Max would sell the company and he'd lose everything he'd worked so hard to steal."

She thought about the robbery at her foster mother's place more than a decade ago and wondered if it would be possible for someone to be so deceitful and duplicitous for so long.

Yeah. Unfortunately, when it came to Leo Gallagher, she believed it was possible.

"Leo was standing right there last week when you said your foster mother had some documents she was going to mail you," Troy said. "He probably panicked and came up here, trying to intercept the package."

"You think his P.I. was the guy who spooked Joe at Flanagan's?" When Troy nodded, she continued speculating. "And the DNA test...he probably did have someone lined up to falsify it. To make it turn out exactly the way he wanted it." She lowered her voice, shaking her head in disgust. "He would have used me, or bribed me. Either way, he never intended to let me find out the truth."

Troy cupped her face and brushed a few tears off her cheek. "Are you all right?"

She nodded. "A little numb. A little shocked." She bit her lip, thinking of all the lost time. "A lot sad."

He obviously understood, not finding it strange that the truth would seem so incredibly tragic to her. Then again, Troy truly cared for Max, too. So maybe his first thought, like hers, had been for all the years they'd wasted. Those years had made Venus stronger, helped mold her into the woman she'd become. But they'd been awfully lonely for Max Longotti.

"Troy, will you take me home tomorrow?"

He nodded. "I'd do anything for you, Venus. Anything."

She stared into his eyes, knowing he meant it. This man, this wonderfully wicked man, loved her with every ounce of his big bad heart.

As she did him.

She smiled and kissed him, almost in awe that she'd been given back the people she most wanted, all within a matter of hours. Troy. Her father. And her grandfather.

Still wrapped safely in the arms of the man she loved, she reached for the phone. "Max?" she said when the old man answered. "It's Venus." She took a deep breath and blinked back fresh tears.

"And," she told him softly, "it's Violet."

* * * * *

Who can resist a bad girl?
Watch for wicked Sydney Colburn's story, in

BRAZEN & BURNING,

by Julie Elizabeth Leto,
coming in March from Temptation.

And finally learn all about
what makes Nicole Bennett tick, in

RED-HOT & RECKLESS,

by Tori Carrington,
coming in April.

THE BAD GIRLS CLUB.

Membership has its privileges!

They're strong, they're sexy, they're not afraid to use the assets Mother Nature gave them....

Venus Messina is...

#916 **WICKED & WILLING**
by Leslie Kelly
February 2003

Sydney Colburn is...

#920 **BRAZEN & BURNING**
by Julie Elizabeth Leto
March 2003

Nicole Bennett is...

#924 **RED-HOT & RECKLESS**
by Tori Carrington
April 2003

The Bad Girls Club...where membership has its privileges!

Available wherever

is sold....

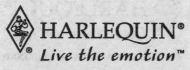

Live the emotion™

Visit us at www.eHarlequin.com

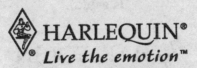

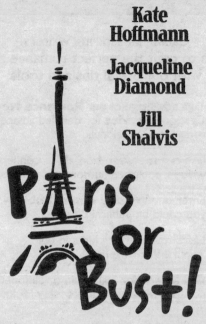